BEST FRIEND
TO WIFE
AND MOTHER?

BEST FRIEND TO WIFE AND MOTHER?

BY

CAROLINE ANDERSON

First published in Great Britain 2015
by Mills & Boon, an imprint of Harlequin (UK) Limited,
Large Print edition 2015
Eton House, 18-24 Paradise Road,
Richmond, Surrey, TW9 1SR

ISBN: 978-0-263-25647-5

Harlequin (UK) Limited's policy is to use papers that are natural, renewable and recyclable products and made from wood grown in sustainable forests. The logging and manufacturing processes conform to the legal environmental regulations of the country of origin.

Printed and bound in Great Britain
by CPI Antony Rowe, Chippenham, Wiltshire

Huge thanks to Caroline and Adam,
and Bryony and Owen, who inadvertently
gave me wonderful wedding inspiration,
and to Shirley and Roger, Mike and Trice,
who invited us to share those days
with them. I love you all.

CHAPTER ONE

'ARE YOU READY?'

He eased a flyaway strand of hair from the corner of her eye, his touch as light as a butterfly's wing, his fingertips lingering for a moment as their eyes met and held. His voice, as familiar to her as her own, was steady and reassuring, but his words didn't reassure her. They sent her mind into free-fall.

They were such simple words, on the surface, but layered beneath were a million unasked and unanswered questions. Questions Leo probably didn't even know he'd asked her. Questions she'd needed to ask herself for months but somehow hadn't got round to.

Was she ready?

For the wedding, yes. The planning had been meticulous, nothing left to chance. Her mother, quietly and efficiently, had seen to that. But the marriage—the *lifetime*—with Nick?

Mingling with the birdsong and the voices of

the people clustered outside the church gates were the familiar strains of the organ music.

The overture for her wedding.

No. Her *marriage.* Subtle difference, but hugely significant.

Amy glanced through the doorway of the church and caught the smiles on the row of faces in the back pew, all of them craning their necks to get a better look at her. The villagers at the gate were mostly there for Leo, hoping to catch a glimpse of their favourite son, but these people in the church—her friends, Nick's—were here to see her marry Nick.

Today.

Right now.

Her heart skittered under the fitted bodice that suddenly seemed so tight she could hardly breathe.

I can't do this—!

No choice. Too late now for cold feet. If she'd been going to change her mind she should have done it ages ago, before the wheels of this massive train that was her wedding had been set in motion. Or later, at a push—but not now, so late it was about to hit the buffers.

The church was full, the food cooked, the champagne on ice. And Nick would be standing at the altar, waiting for her.

Dear, kind, lovely Nick, who'd been there for her when her life had been in chaos, who'd just—been there, for the last three years, her friend and companion and cheerleader. Her lover. And she did love him. She did…

Enough to marry him? Till death us do part, and all that? Or is it just the easiest thing to do?

You can *stop this,* the voice whispered in her head. *It's not too late.*

But it was. Way too late. She was marrying Nick.

Today.

A curious calm settled over her, as if a switch had been flicked, turning on the autopilot, steadying her fall into oblivion. The voice in her head didn't care.

Just because it's easy, because you know he'll be a good husband and father and he's safe? Is that enough?

Of course it was enough. It was just nerves unsettling her. That was all. Last-minute nerves. Nick was—fine.

Fine? Like safe, steady, reliable, predictable—

that kind of fine? No chemistry, no fireworks? And whatever happened to amazing?

She tuned the voice out. There were more important things than amazing. Trust, fidelity, respect—and chemistry was overrated—

How do you know that? You don't *know that. You haven't got a clue, you've never felt it. And if you marry Nick, you never will...*

She stifled the voice again, stuffing it firmly back in its box; then, easing her death grip on the bouquet, she straightened her shoulders, tilted up her chin and gave Leo her most convincing and dazzling smile.

'Yes,' she said firmly. 'I'm ready.'

Leo felt his breath catch at that smile.

When had she grown up? Turned into this stunningly lovely woman, instead of the slightly chubby, relentlessly accident-prone girl who'd dogged his footsteps for ever? He'd turned his back for what felt like five minutes, and she'd been transformed.

More like five years, though, give or take, and a lot of water under the bridge for both of them. Far too much, in his case, and so much of it tainted by regret.

He cradled her pale cheek in his hand, and felt her quiver. She was nervous. Of course she was. Who wouldn't be, on their wedding day? It was a hell of a commitment. Literally, in his case.

'You look beautiful, Amy,' he said gruffly, looking down into the wide grey eyes of this lovely young woman he'd known so well but now hardly knew at all. 'He's a lucky man.'

'Thank you.'

Her eyes searched his, a flicker of uncertainty in them echoing the tiny tremor in her cheek, the smile on her lush, pink lips a little hesitant now, and he felt himself frown.

Second thoughts? About time. There was nothing wrong with the man she was marrying, from what little he'd seen of him—in fact, he'd liked him, a lot—but they just didn't seem *right* for each other.

There was no chemistry between them, no zing that he could see. Maybe she didn't want that? Maybe she just wanted safe and comfortable? And maybe that was a really, really good idea.

Or maybe not, not for Amy…

He hesitated another second, then took her hand in his, his thumb slowly stroking the back of it in a subconscious gesture of comfort. Her fingers were cold, trembling slightly in his, reinforcing his concern. He squeezed them gently.

'Amy, I'm going to ask you something. It's only what your father would have done, so please don't take it the wrong way, but—are you sure you want to do this? Because if not, you can still turn around and walk away. It's your life, no one else's, and nobody else can decide this for you.'

His voice dropped, his frown deepening as he struggled to get the importance of this across to her before it was too late. If only someone had done this for him…

'Don't do it unless it's right, Amy, unless you really, truly love him. Take it from me, marrying the wrong person for the wrong reasons is a recipe for disaster. You have to be absolutely, completely and utterly sure that it's the right thing to do and for the right reasons.'

A shadow flitted across her eyes, her fingers tightening on his, and after an infinitesimal pause that seemed to last an eternity, she nodded. 'Yes. Yes, of course I'm sure.'

But she didn't look sure, and he certainly wasn't, but it was nothing to do with him, was it? Not his decision to make. And the shadows in her eyes could just as easily be sadness because her much-loved father wasn't here to give her away. Nothing to do with her choice of groom…

Not your business who she chooses to love. God knows, you're no expert. And he could be a lot, lot worse.

He hauled in a breath.

'OK. Ready to go, then?'

She nodded, but he saw her swallow again, and for a moment he wondered if she'd changed her mind.

And then she straightened up and took a breath, hooked her hand through his arm and flashed a smile over her shoulder at her bridesmaids. 'OK, girls? Good to go?'

They both nodded, and he felt her hand tighten on his arm.

'OK, then. Let's do this.' Her eyes flicked up and met Leo's, her fake smile pinned in place by sheer determination, but it didn't waver and anybody else might have been convinced.

Not your business. He nodded to the usher, who nodded to the organist, and after a moment's silence, broken only by the shuffling of the congregation getting to their feet and the clearing of a few throats, the evocative strains of Pachelbel's *Canon in D Major* filled the church.

He laid his hand over hers, squeezed her fingers and felt them grip his. He glanced down, into those liquid grey eyes that seemed flooded with doubt despite the brave smile, and his gut clenched.

He'd known her for ever, rescued her from a million scrapes, both literal and otherwise; dammit, she was his best friend, or had been before the craziness that was his life had got in the way, and he couldn't bear to see her make the mistake of her life.

Don't do it, Amy. Please, don't do it!

'It's still not too late,' he said gruffly, his voice muted, his head tilted towards her so only she could hear.

'Yes, it is,' she said, so softly he barely heard her, then she dredged up that expected smile again and took the first step forward.

Damn.

He swallowed the lump in his throat and slowly, steadily, walked her down the aisle.

With every step, her legs felt heavier and more reluctant, her heart pounding, the sense of unease settling closer around her, chilling her to the bone.

What are you doing?

Nick was there, watching her thoughtfully. Warily?

It's still not too late.

She felt Leo ease his arm out from under her hand and step away, and she felt—abandoned?

It was her wedding day. She should feel a sense of joy, of completeness, of utter, bone-deep rightness—but she didn't.

Not at all.

And, as she glanced up at Nick, she realised that neither did he. Either that, or he was paralysed by nerves, which was unlikely. He wasn't remotely the nervous type.

He took her hand briefly, squeezed it in reassurance, but it felt wrong. So wrong...

She eased it away, using the excuse of handing her bouquet to the waiting bridesmaid, and then the vicar spoke, everyone started to sing 'Jerusalem', and she felt her mouth move automatically while her mind whirled. *Her mind*, this time, not the voice in her head giving her grief, or a moment of panic, stage fright, last-minute nerves or whatever. This time it was really her, finally asking all the questions Leo's 'Are you ready?' had prompted.

What are we doing*? And why? Who for?*

The last echoes of the hymn filtered away, and the vicar did the just cause or impediment bit. *Was* there a just cause? Was not loving him enough sufficient? And then she saw the vicar's lips move as he began to speak the words of the marriage service, drowned out by her thudding heart and the whirlwind in her head.

Until he said, 'Who gives this woman to be married to this man?' and Leo stepped forward, took her hand with a tiny, barely perceptible squeeze, and gave it—gave her—to Nick.

Dear Nick. Lovely, kind, dependable Nick, ready to make her his wife, give her the babies they both longed for, grow old with her…

But Nick hesitated. When the vicar asked if he would take this woman to be his wife, he hesitated. And then—was that a shrug?—his mouth twisted in a wry smile and he said, 'I will.'

The vicar turned, spoke to her, but she wasn't really listening any more. She was staring into Nick's eyes, searching them for the truth, and all she could see was duty.

Duty from him, and duty from her? Because they'd come this far before either of them had realised it was bound to be—what were Leo's words?—a disaster?

She gripped his hands. 'Will you? Will you *re-ally*?' she asked under her breath. 'Because I'm not sure I can.'

Behind her she heard the slight suck of Leo's indrawn breath, the rustle from the congregation, the whispered undertone of someone asking what she'd said.

And then Nick smiled—the first time he'd re-ally smiled at her in weeks, she realised—and put his arms around her, and hugged her against his broad, solid chest. It shook with what could have been a huff of laughter, and he squeezed her tight.

His breath brushed her cheek, his words soft in her ear. 'You cut that a bit fine, my love.'

She felt the tension flow out of her like air out of a punctured balloon, and if he hadn't been hold-ing her she would have crumpled.

'I did, didn't I? I'm sorry, Nick, but I just can't do this,' she murmured.

'I know; it doesn't feel right, does it? I thought it would, but…it just doesn't. And better now than later.' She felt his arms slacken as he raised his head and looked over her shoulder.

'Time to go, sweetheart,' he murmured, his mouth tugging into a wistful smile. 'Leo's wait-ing for you. He'll make sure you're all right.' He kissed her gently on the cheek and stepped back, his smile a little unsteady now. 'Be happy, Amy.'

She searched his eyes, and saw regret and relief, and her eyes welled with tears. 'You, too,' she said silently, and took a step back, then another one, and collided with Leo's solid warmth.

His hands cupped her elbows, supporting her as everything slowly righted itself. She turned to him, met those steady golden eyes and whispered, 'Thank you.'

And then she picked up her skirts and ran.

She'd done it. She'd actually done it. Walked—no, sprinted, or as close to it as she could in those ridiculous shoes—away from disaster.

Leo watched her go, her mother and bridesmaids hurrying after her, watched Nick turn to his best man and sit down on the pew behind him as if his strings had been cut, and realised it was all down to him. Appropriate, really, since in a way he was the cause of it.

He hauled in a deep breath, turned to the stunned congregation and gave them his best media smile.

'Ladies and gentlemen, it seems there isn't going to be a wedding today after all. I'm not sure of the protocol for this kind of thing, but there's food ready and waiting for you in the marquee, and any of you who'd like to come back and enjoy it will be more than welcome to do so before you head off. I gather the chef comes highly recommended,' he added drily, and there was a ripple of laughter that broke the tension.

He nodded to his father, who nodded back, pulling his mobile phone out of his pocket to set the ball rolling with their catering team, and with a brief nod to the vicar, Leo strode swiftly down the aisle and out of the church after Amy.

The sun warmed him, the gentle rays bringing the life back into his limbs, and he realised he'd been stone cold at the prospect of watching her make a disastrous mistake. He flexed his fingers as he walked over to the vintage Bentley and peered inside.

She was in there, perched on the seat in a billowing cloud of tulle and lace, surrounded by her mother and bridesmaids all clucking like mother hens, and the villagers gathered around the gate were agog. As well they might be.

He ducked his head inside the car.

'Amy?' he murmured, and she stared blankly up at him. She looked lost, shocked and confused and just a little crazy, and he could read the desperate appeal in her eyes.

'Take her home, I'll follow,' he instructed the driver tersely, and as the car whisked her away one of the crowd at the gate yelled, 'What's going on, Leo?'

He didn't answer. They could see what was going on, they just didn't know why, and he had better things to do than stand around and tittle-tattle. He turned to scan the throng of puzzled guests spilling out of the church, milling aimlessly around, unsure of what to do next, and in the midst of them he found his parents heading towards him.

'Is she all right?' his mother asked worriedly, and he nodded.

'I think so. She will be. Let's get out of here. We've got things to do.'

She'd done it.

Stopped the train and run away—from Nick, from the certainty of her carefully planned and mapped-out future, from everything that made up her life, and she felt lost. Cast adrift, swamped by a million conflicting emotions, unsure of what to do or think or feel.

Actually, she couldn't feel anything much. Just numbness, a sort of strange hollowness deep in her chest as if there was nothing there any more.

Better than the ice-cold dread of doing the wrong thing, but not much.

She tugged off her veil, handing it to her bridesmaids. If she could she would have taken the dress off, too, there and then. She couldn't get out of it fast enough. Couldn't get out of all of it fast enough, the church, the dress, the car—the country?

She almost laughed, but the hysteria bubbling in her throat threatened to turn to tears so she clamped her teeth shut and crushed it ruthlessly down. Not now. Not yet.

'Are you all right, darling?' Her mother's face was troubled but calm, and Amy heaved a shaky sigh of relief. At least she wasn't going off the deep end. Not that her mother was a deep-end kind of person, but you never knew. And her daughter hadn't ever jilted anyone at the altar before, so the situation wasn't exactly tried and tested.

'Yes, I'm fine. I'm really sorry, Mum.'

'Don't be. It's the first sensible thing you've done for months.'

Amy stared at her, astonished. 'I thought you liked him?'

'I do like him! He's lovely. I just don't think he's right for you. You don't have that spark.'

Not her, too, joining in with her alter ego and reminding her she'd been about to do the wrong thing for the wrong reasons and should have pulled out much, much earlier.

Or he should. Both of them, for everyone's sake. Oh, what a mess!

The car door opened, and she realised they'd come to rest on the drive. Gathering up her skirts, she climbed awkwardly out and headed for the front door. Her mother unlocked it and pushed it open and Amy was swept inside on the tide of her redundant bridesmaids, into the hallway of the house she'd left such a short time before as a bride on the brink of a nice, safe, sensible marriage. Now she was—she didn't know what she was.

A runaway bride?

Such a cliché. She gave a smothered laugh and shook her head.

'I need to get out of this dress,' she muttered, kicking off her shoes and heading for the stairs and the sanctuary of her bedroom.

'I'll come,' her mother said, and they all fell in behind her, threatening to suffocate her with kindness.

She paused on the third stair and turned back. 'No, Mum. Actually, none of you. I think I'd like to be alone for a moment.'

They ground to a halt, three pairs of worried eyes studying her. Checking to see if she'd lost her marbles, probably. Wrong. She'd just found them, at the absolutely last minute. *Oh, Nick, I'm sorry...*

'Are you sure you're all right?' her mother asked, her face creased with concern.

'Yes,' she said, more firmly this time. 'Yes, I'm sure.' Sure about everything except what her future held. 'Don't worry, I'm not going to do anything stupid.' Or at least, nothing as stupid as marrying the wrong man would have been. Not that she knew who the right one was, or how she'd recognise him. She seemed to have a gift for getting it wrong.

They were all still standing there as if they didn't know what to do now their carefully planned schedule had been thrown out the window, but it was no good asking her. She didn't have a clue. She turned back to the stairs, putting one foot in front of the other, skirts bunched in her quivering hands.

'Shall I bring you up a cup of tea?' her mother asked, breaking the silence.

Tea. Of course. The universal panacea. And it would give her mother something to do. 'That would be lovely, Mum. Whenever you're ready. Don't rush.'

'I'll put the kettle on.'

Her mother disappeared into the kitchen, the bridesmaids trailing in her wake as one after the other they came out of their trances, and she made it to the safety of her bedroom and shut the door before the bubble burst and the first tears fell.

Odd, that she was crying when she felt so little. It was just a release of tension, but without the tension there was nothing, just a yawning chasm opening up in front of her, and she thought she was going to fall apart. Pressing her hand to her mouth to stifle the sobs, she slid down the door, crumpling to the floor in a billowing cloud of lace and petticoats, and let the floodgates open.

He had to get to her.

He could only imagine what state she was in,

but that look in her eyes when she'd glanced up in the car—

He pulled up on the driveway of his family home, and after checking that the baby was all right and the catering was under control he headed through the gate in the fence into Amy's garden and tapped on the kitchen door.

Amy's mother let him in, her face troubled. 'Oh, Leo, I'm so glad you're here,' she said, and hugged him briefly, her composure wobbling for a second.

'How is she?' he asked.

'I don't know. She's gone upstairs. She wouldn't let us go—said she needed to be alone. I've made her a cup of tea, I was just about to take it up.'

'Give it to me. I'll go and talk to her. This is my fault.'

'Your fault?'

He gave her a wry smile. 'I asked her if she was sure.'

Jill smiled back at him and kissed his cheek. 'Well, thank God you did, Leo. I haven't had the guts. Here, take it. And get her out of here, can you? She doesn't need all this hoopla.'

He nodded, took the tea and headed for the stairs. Her bedroom was over the kitchen, with a perfect view of the marquee on his parents' lawn and the steady stream of guests who were arriving for the wedding reception that wasn't.

Damn.

He crossed the landing and tapped on her bedroom door.

Someone was knocking.

Her mother, probably. She dropped her head back against the door and sucked in a breath. She wasn't ready to face her. Wasn't ready to face anyone—

'Amy? Can I come in?'

Leo. Her mother must have sent him up. She heard the knob turn, could feel the door gently pushing her in the back, but she couldn't move. Didn't want to move. She wanted to stay there for ever, hiding from everyone, until she'd worked out what had happened and what she was going to do with the rest of her life.

His voice came through the door again, low and gentle. 'Amy? Let me in, sweetheart. I've got a cup of tea for you.'

It was the tea that made her move. That, and the reassuring normality of his voice. She shuffled over, hauling her voluminous skirts with her, and he pushed the door gently inwards until he could squeeze past it and shut it behind him.

She sniffed hard, and she heard him tutting softly. He crouched down, his face coming into view, his eyes scanning the mess her face must be. She scrubbed her cheeks with her hands and he held out a wad of tissues.

He'd even come prepared, she thought, and the tears began again.

She heard the soft click of his tongue as he tutted again, the gentle touch of his hand on her hair. 'Oh, Amy.'

He put the tea down, sat on the floor next to her and hauled her into his arms. 'Come here, you silly thing. You'll be OK. It'll all work out in the end.'

'Will it? How? What am I going to do?' she mumbled into his shoulder, busily shredding the sodden tissues in her lap. 'I've given up my job, I'd already given up my flat—we were about to move out of his flat and buy a family house and have babies, and I was going to try going freelance with my photography, and now…I don't have a life any more, Leo. It's all gone, every part of it. I just walked away from it and I feel as if I've stepped off a cliff. I must be mad!'

Leo's heart contracted.

Poor Amy. She sounded utterly lost, and it tugged at something deep inside him, some part of him that had spent years protecting her from the fallout of her impulsive nature. He hugged her closer, rocking her gently against his chest. 'I don't think you're mad. I think it's the first sensible thing you've done in ages,' he told her gently, echoing her mother's words.

She shifted so she could see his face. 'How come everybody else knew this except me?' she said plaintively. 'Why am I so stupid?'

'You aren't stupid. He's a nice guy. He's just not the right man for you. If he was, you wouldn't have hesitated for a moment, and nor would he. And it didn't seem to me as if you'd broken his heart. Quite the opposite.'

'No.' There'd been nothing heartbroken, she thought, about the flash of relief in his eyes in that fleeting moment. Sadness, yes, but no heartbreak. 'I suppose he was just doing the decent thing.'

Leo's eyes clouded and he turned away. 'Yeah. Trust me, it doesn't work.'

'Was that what you did?' she asked him, momentarily distracted from her own self-induced catastrophe. 'The decent thing? When you married the wrong person for the wrong reasons?'

A muscle bunched in his jaw. 'Something like that. Are you going to drink this tea or not?'

She took the mug that he was holding out to her, cradled it in both hands and sighed shakily.

'You OK now?'

She nodded. She was, she realised. Just about, so long as she didn't have to make any more decisions, because clearly she was unqualified in that department. She sipped her tea, lifted her head and rested it back against the wall with another shaky little sigh. 'I will be. I don't know; I just feel—I can't explain—as if I can't trust myself any more. I don't know who I am, and I thought I knew. Does that make sense, Leo?'

'Absolutely. Been there, done that, worn out the T-shirt.'

She turned to him, searching his face and finding only kindness and concern. No reproach. No disappointment in her. Just Leo, doing what he always did, getting her out of the mess she'd got herself into.

Again.

'Leo, will you get me out of here?' she asked unevenly. 'I can't stay here, not with all this...'

'Of course I will. That's what I'm here for.'

'To rescue me? Poor you. I bet you thought you were done with all that at last.'

'What, me? Change the habits of a lifetime?' he teased, and she had to laugh, even though it wasn't really remotely funny.

She glanced down at herself, then at him. He'd abandoned the tailcoat, loosened the rose-pink cravat which showed off his olive skin to perfection, and turned back the cuffs on his immaculate white shirt to reveal strong wrists above hands criss-crossed with fine white scars. Chef's hands, he called them, but the scars didn't detract from his appeal, not in any way. He'd been fighting girls off with a stick since he'd hit puberty, and the scars hadn't put them off at all.

She managed a small smile. 'We might have to change first, before we go.'

His lips quirked. 'You think? I thought I looked rather good like this.'

So did she, but then she thought he looked good in anything.

'You do, but if the press catch a glimpse of us, they'll think the nation's favourite celebrity chef's secretly tied the knot again,' she said, her mouth on autopilot, and his face clouded.

'Yeah, well, it'll be a cold day in hell before that ever happens,' he said tightly, and she could have kicked herself for blundering all over such a sensitive area. She closed her eyes and let out an anguished sigh.

'Oh, God, Leo, I'm so sorry. I can't believe I said that—'

'It's OK, it doesn't matter, and you're quite right. I don't need that sort of publicity, and neither do you.' He smiled fleetingly, then looked away again. 'So, anywhere in particular you want to go?'

'I don't know. Got any ideas?'

He shrugged. 'Not really. My house is still crawling with builders, and I have to fly to Tuscany tomorrow on business.'

'Oh.' Her heart sank at the thought of him going, and she felt her smile slip. 'I don't suppose you want to smuggle me out there in your luggage?' she joked weakly, and propped up her wavering smile. 'I promise not to be a nuisance.'

'How many times have I heard you say that?' he murmured drily, and she felt a wash of guilt flood over her.

He was right—she was always imposing on him, getting him to extract her from one mess or another. Or she had done, back in the days when they really had been best friends. And that was years ago.

She forced herself to ease away from him, to stop leaning on him, both metaphorically and physically. Time to get out her big girl pants and put their friendship on a more equal and adult footing.

She scraped up the last smile in the bottom of the bucket and plastered it on her face.

'I'm sorry, I was only joking. I know you can't. Don't worry about me, Leo, I'll be all right. It's my mess, I'll clear it up.'

Somehow…

CHAPTER TWO

HE COULDN'T DO IT.

He couldn't desert her when her life had just turned upside down—and anyway, it might well be the perfect solution for both of them.

He'd been worrying about leaving tomorrow and abandoning her with the repercussions of all this, worrying about how he was going to juggle his tiny daughter and business meetings, and here was the answer, on a plate. Unless…

He studied her thoughtfully, searching her face for clues. '*Were* you joking about coming with me? Because if not, it could be a great idea. Not the smuggling, obviously, but if you did it could solve both our problems.'

A tiny frown appeared. 'You've got a problem?'

He nodded. 'Sort of. I've got meetings to go to, and business and babies don't mix. Normally I'd leave Ella behind with my parents, but this is going to be for several days and it's not fair on them at their age, especially on top of the wedding—and don't say it,' he added, pressing a finger lightly on her lips to stifle the apology he knew was coming.

She took hold of his hand and moved it away. 'Why not, since it's true? It *is* my fault, and they've gone to so much trouble—'

He pulled his hand back and placed it firmly over her mouth to silence her before she got back onto that again.

'I don't want to argue, Amy. Hear me out. Please?'

She nodded, and he lowered his hand and carried on. 'I like to be there for Ella every day, even if it's only for part of it, even if it means dragging her around with me. It's the only way I've been able to look after her and my business, and it's a precarious balance that so far seems to be working. I don't want to upset that balance, abandon her for days and nights on end—and anyway, shortly after I get back I start filming the next TV series for eight weeks or so, and I'm going to need my parents' goodwill for that. If you would come to Italy with us and look after her just while I'm in the meetings, it would be amazingly helpful.'

Amy eyed him thoughtfully. 'Really? You mean it? I *was* only joking, really. I didn't expect you to say yes. I was just trying to—I don't know. Make light of it, really. I don't want to be a burden to you.'

'Absolutely I mean it, and you wouldn't be a burden. Not at all. You'd be a real help. I'm trying to set up a contract with a family there to supply our restaurants. I tasted some of their products at a trade fair, and I was really impressed. I want to see how they operate, taste the whole range, negotiate the price and see if we can strike a deal. And doing all that with Ella on my hip *really* won't work.'

She laughed a little wryly. 'No, I can see that. Not exactly professional, and not really fair on her, either.'

'No, it isn't, and she's my top priority. If necessary, I'd cut the trip short rather than compromise my relationship with her, but I don't want to have to do that, because this is a really great business opportunity and it could be important for her future as well as mine.

'So—will you come? You'll have lots of free time to take photos, and it's beautiful at this time of year. You can chill out away from all this, get some thinking time, clear your head, work out what you're going to do next. Maybe work on a portfolio of images, if that's where you think you're going.'

It sounded tempting. Very tempting, and she could see that he quite genuinely needed her help. He wasn't just making it up—and anyway, even if he was, did she have a better choice? No. And to stay here another minute was unthinkable.

She could hear the sounds of people thronging outside in the garden—not their garden, but his parents' garden next door, where the marquee had been set up for the reception.

Her hand flew to her mouth, her eyes locked on his. 'Oh, Leo! All that food…!'

She was swamped with guilt, but he shook his head briskly, brushing it aside as if it was nothing. Which it wasn't, far from it.

'It's not wasted. There are lots of people there to eat it, it's fine.'

'Fine?' It wasn't fine. Nothing was fine, and all of a sudden she was overwhelmed again. 'It was supposed to be a *wedding* present from you, and I didn't even *have* the wedding.'

'Oh, Amy,' he sighed, and pulled her head back down against his shoulder, soothing her as the tears spilled down her cheeks yet again and the enormity of what she'd done, the chaos she'd caused, the things she'd walked away from, gradually sank in and left her breathless with guilt and remorse.

'I can't even pay you back,' she choked out, but he tutted softly and cradled her head against that solid, familiar shoulder that felt so good she could have stayed there for ever.

'Hush. You don't need to. Forget it, Amy, it's the least important thing in the world right now. Don't worry about it.'

She pushed herself up, swiping the tears off her cheeks with her palms. 'But I *am* worried about it! At least let me pay you back for it when I get a job.'

If she ever did. Publishing was in a state of flux, and she'd just walked away from a great career in a really good publishing house because she'd thought she'd have financial security with Nick and could afford to try freelancing with her photography, and now she had nothing! No job, no home, no husband, no future—and all because of some vague sense of unease? She must have been mad—

'OK, so here's the deal,' he said, cutting off her tumbling thoughts with a brisk, no-nonsense tone. 'Come to Tuscany with me. Look after Ella while I'm in meetings, so I can work all day with a clear conscience and still put her to bed every night, and we'll call it quits.'

'*Quits*? Are you *crazy*? I know what your outside catering costs, Leo!'

He gave her a wry grin. 'There's a substantial mark-up. The true cost is nothing like the tariff. And you know how precious my daughter is to me. Nothing could be more important than leaving her with someone I can trust while I'm over there.'

He gripped her hands, his eyes fixed on hers. 'Come with us, look after her while I'm in meetings, have a holiday, some time out while you work out what to do next. And take photos for me—pictures of me cooking, of the produce, the region, the markets—all of it. Your photos are brilliant, and I can use them for my blog. That would be really valuable to me, so much more professional, and certainly something I'd pay good money for. I usually do it myself and blag people into taking photos of me with chefs and market traders and artisans, and if I'm really stuck I get reduced to taking selfies, and that's *so* not a good look!'

She laughed, a funny little sound between a

chuckle and a sob that she quickly stifled, and he hugged her again.

'Come on. Do this for me—please? It would be so helpful I can't tell you, and it'll get you away from all this. You're exhausted and you need to get away, have a total change of scene. And I need you, Amy. I'm not making it up. Not for the photos, they're just a valuable added bonus, but for Ella, and I can't put a price on her safety and happiness.'

She searched his eyes again, and saw behind the reassuringly calm exterior that he was telling her the truth. He wasn't just being kind to her, he really was in a jam, and he'd never ever asked her for help, although God knows he'd given her enough over the years, bailing her out of umpteen scrapes.

Not to mention the catering.

No. She had no choice—and she realised she didn't want a choice. She wanted to be with Leo. His sound common sense was exactly what she needed to get her through this, and let's face it, she thought, he's had enough practice at dealing with me and my appalling life choices.

She nodded. 'OK. I'll come—of course I'll come, and I'll help you with Ella and take photos and do whatever else I can while you're there. It'll be a pleasure to help you, and it's high time I gave you something back. On one condition, though.'

'Which is?' he asked warily.

'I help you with her care when the filming starts—take some of the burden off your parents. Then I'll call it quits.'

'That's a big commitment.'

'I know that, but that's the deal. Take it or leave it.'

His shoulders dropped, relief written all over him, and she felt some of the tension leave her, too.

'I'll take it. And thank you, Amy. Thank you so much.' His brow furrowed. 'Do you have a case packed ready to go?'

'Yes. I've got smart-casual, beach, jeans—will that do?'

He nodded and got to his feet. 'Sounds fine. I'll get Ella's stuff together and we'll go. I'm not sure, but we might even be able to fly out today.'

'Today!'

'Is that a problem?'

She shook her head vehemently. 'No. Not at all. The sooner the better. I was just surprised. I thought you said you were going tomorrow.'

'I was, but today would be better and I seem to be unexpectedly free now,' he added, that wry grin tugging at his mouth and making her want to hug him. 'I'll see what I can do. How soon can you be ready?'

She shrugged. 'Half an hour? Twenty minutes, maybe?'

'OK. I'll call if there's a problem. Don't forget your passport—and your camera.'

'In my bag. Just do one thing for me before you go. Get me out of this dress? I'd forgotten all the stupid buttons.'

She scrambled to her feet and turned her back to him, and he began undoing the million and one tiny satin buttons and loops that covered the zip underneath. And as he worked, button by button, he became suddenly, intensely aware of the smooth, creamy skin of her shoulders, the fine line of her neck, the slender column of her throat. He could see a pulse beating under the skin at the side, and feel the tension coming off her. Off him, too, but for an entirely different reason. Crazy. This was Amy, for goodness' sake! She was his childhood best friend, virtually his sister!

He finally freed the last button and slid the concealed zip down, and she caught the dress against her chest and turned to face him, a peep of cleavage above some transparent lacy undergarment taking him by surprise. He hauled his eyes up away from it, shocked by the sudden heat that flared through his body.

Really?

Amy?

He backed up a step. 'OK now?' he asked tersely, his throat tight.

'Yes. Thank you. I'll get changed and see you downstairs in a few minutes.'

'Good. Wear something comfortable for travelling.' Preferably something that covered her up. He backed away further, turning on his heel and reaching for the door handle, suddenly desperate to get out of there.

'Leo?'

Her voice checked him and he turned and looked at her over his shoulder, raising an eyebrow in question.

'I'm starving. Grab some food to take with us, would you?'

Food? He laughed, letting some of the tension go. Food was easy. Food he could do.

'Sure. See you in a bit.'

He called the catering manager on the way down

the stairs, rang his mother to prime her and went into the kitchen.

Three pairs of eyes locked on him instantly. 'How is she?'

'She'll do. Jill, can you help her get ready? I'm taking her to Tuscany with me and we're leaving as soon as possible. I'm trying to get a flight this afternoon.'

'Tuscany? Brilliant, it's just what she needs.' She went up on tiptoe and kissed his cheek. 'Thank you, Leo. Bless you. She'll be ready.'

It was tight.

While he packed he rang the charter company he used from time to time, and found they had a small jet flying to Florence for a pick-up; he could hire the whole plane for the 'empty leg' rate, but it was leaving City Airport at three. And it was twelve forty already.

Tight, but doable, if she was ready to go. He rang to warn her, loaded the car in no time flat and drove straight round there, reaching the front door as Amy opened it.

'I'm ready,' she said, her smile a little forced in her pale face, her eyes still red-rimmed, but there was life in them now, unlike the blank eyes of the woman he'd walked down the aisle less than an hour ago. Sure, she was hanging by a thread, but she'd make it, especially once he'd got her out of here, and he was suddenly fiercely glad that he'd managed to convince her to come with him.

'Got your passport?'

'Yes, I've got everything. What's the luggage limit?'

He smiled wryly. 'There isn't one. It's a private charter.'

Her jaw dropped slightly. 'Private—?'

He pushed her chin up gently with an index finger and smiled at her stunned expression. 'It's going on an empty leg to pick someone up—I'm only paying a fraction of the normal charge.' Which was still extortionate, but she didn't need to know that.

'Wow. Great. OK.' She turned to her mother, hugged her hard, hugged her bridesmaids and got in the car.

'Thank you, Leo,' Jill called, and he lifted a hand as he slid behind the wheel and closed the door.

'Did you get food?' Amy asked, and he leant over into the back and pulled out an insulated bag. 'Here. You can feed me en route.'

'Or I might just eat it all.'

'Piglet. Buckle up,' he instructed, but she was there already, her bottom lip caught between her teeth, the eyes that kept flicking to his filled with a welter of emotions that he couldn't begin to analyse. He didn't suppose she could, either, but there seemed to be a glimmer of something that could have been excitement.

He smiled at her, and she smiled back, but it was a fleeting parody of her usual open, happy smile, and he felt another sudden pang of guilt. What if it wasn't excitement? What if it was hysteria? She was on a knife-edge, he knew that. Had he imposed his own feelings about marriage on her? Put doubts in her mind when they hadn't really been there at all? He hoped not—even if Nick hadn't been right for her, it wasn't his call to sabotage their wedding.

'You OK?'

She nodded. 'Yes—or I will be, just as soon as we get out of here.'

'Let's go, then,' he said, and starting the engine he pulled smoothly off the drive and headed for London.

Amy had never flown in such luxury.

From start to finish, boarding the little jet had

been a breeze. They'd driven right up to the Jet Centre terminal, their luggage and the baby's car seat and buggy were handed over, and the car had been whisked away to secure parking. The security check-in was thorough but almost instant, and then they had a short walk to the plane.

At the top of the steps the pilot greeted them by name as he welcomed them aboard, gave them their ETA, a benign weather report and told them there was a car waiting for them at Florence. Then he disappeared through the galley area into the cockpit and closed the door, leaving them with the entire little jet to themselves, and for the first time she registered her surroundings.

'Wow.' She felt her jaw dropping slightly, and no wonder. It was like another world, a world she'd never entered before or even dreamed of.

There were no endless rows of seating, no central aisle barely wide enough to pass through, no hard-wearing gaudy seat fabric in a budget airline's colours. Instead, there were two small groups of pale leather seats, the ones at the rear bracketing tables large enough to set up a laptop, play games, eat a meal, or simply flick through a magazine and glance out of the window. And

Ella's car seat was securely strapped in all ready for her.

Leo headed that way and she followed, the tight, dense pile of the carpet underfoot making her feel as if she was walking on air. Maybe she was? Maybe they'd already taken off and she just hadn't noticed? Or maybe it was all part of the weird, dreamlike state she'd been in ever since she'd turned her back on Nick and walked away.

A wave of dizziness washed over her, and she grabbed the back of one of the seats to steady herself and felt Leo's hand at her waist, steering her to a seat at the back of the plane across the aisle from Ella's.

'Sit. And don't argue,' he added firmly.

She didn't argue. She was beyond arguing. She just sat obediently like a well-trained Labrador, sinking into the butter-soft cream leather as her legs gave way, watching him while he strapped little Ella into her seat, his big hands gentle and competent as he assembled the buckle and clicked it firmly into place.

She hoped she never had to do it. It looked extraordinarily complicated for something so simple, and she was suddenly swamped with doubts about her ability to do this.

What on earth did she know about babies? Less than nothing. You could write it all in capitals on the head of a very small pin. He must be nuts to trust her with his child.

She heard voices as a man and woman in uniform came up the steps and into the plane, and moments later the door was shut and the woman was approaching them with a smile, her hand extended.

'Mr Zacharelli.'

Leo shook her hand and returned the smile. 'Julie, isn't it? We've flown together before.'

'We have, sir. It's a pleasure to welcome you and Ella on board again, and Miss Driver, I believe? I'm your cabin crew today, and if there's anything you need, don't hesitate to ask.'

She smiled at Amy as they shook hands, and turned her attention back to Leo.

'May I go through the pre-flight safety procedure with you?' she asked, and he delved into the baby's bag and handed Ella a crackly, brightly coloured dragonfly toy to distract her while Julie launched into the familiar spiel.

It took a few minutes, showing them the overhead oxygen, the emergency exit—all the usual things, but with the massive difference that she was talking only to them, and the smiles she gave were personal. Especially to Leo, Amy thought, and mentally rolled her eyes at yet another effortless conquest on his part. He probably wasn't even aware of it.

And then it was done, another smile flashed in his direction, and Julie took herself off and left them alone.

'Was that from me?' Amy asked, pointing at the dragonfly toy Ella was happily playing with.

Leo nodded, sending her a fleeting smile. 'You sent her it when she was born. She loves it. I have to take it everywhere with us.'

That made her smile. At least she'd done one thing right, then, in the last year or so. He zipped the bag up, stashed it in the baggage compartment, put her hand luggage in there, too, and sat down opposite Ella and across from Amy.

His tawny gold eyes searched hers thoughtfully. 'You OK now?'

If you don't count the butterflies stampeding around in my stomach like a herd of elephants, she thought, but she said nothing, just nodded, and he raised a brow a fraction but didn't comment.

'Do you always travel like this?' she asked, still

slightly stunned by their surroundings but rapidly getting used to it.

He laughed softly. 'Only if I'm travelling with Ella or if time's short. Usually I go business class. It's just much easier with a baby to travel somewhere private. I'm sure you've been in a plane when there's been a screaming baby—like this,' he added, as Ella caught sight of the bottle he'd tried to sneak out of his pocket so he could fasten his seat belt. She reached for it, little hands clenching and unclenching as she started to whimper, and Leo hid the bottle under the table.

'No, *mia bella,* not yet,' he said gently, and the whimper escalated to an indignant wail.

Amy laughed softly. 'Right on cue.'

She propped her elbows on the table and leant towards Ella, smiling at her and waggling her dragonfly in an attempt to distract her.

'Hi, sweet pea,' she crooned softly. 'You aren't really going to scream all the way there, are you? No, of course not!'

Finally distracted from the bottle, Ella beamed at her and squashed the toy. It made a lovely, satisfying noise, so she did it again, and Leo chuckled.

'Babies are refreshingly easy to please. Give them a toy and they're happy.'

'Like men, really. Fast car, big TV, fancy coffee maker...private jet—'

He gave a soft snort and shot her a look. 'Don't push it. And don't get lulled into a false sense of security because you managed to distract her this time. She can be a proper little tyrant if it suits her. You're a monster in disguise, aren't you, *mia bella*?'

He said it with such affection, and Amy's heart turned over. Poor little scrap, losing her mother so young and so tragically. Leo must have been devastated—although not for himself, from what he'd said. He'd told her that marrying the wrong person was a recipe for disaster and it would be a cold day in hell before he did it again, so it didn't sound as if his marriage had been a match made in heaven, by any means. But even so—

'I need to make a quick call to sort out where we're going to stay tonight. Can you entertain her, please, Amy? I won't be a moment.'

'Sure.' Amy shut the door on that avenue of thought and turned her attention to amusing Ella. She'd got enough mess of her own to deal with, without probing into Leo's.

But Ella didn't really need entertaining, not with her dragonfly to chew and crackle, so Amy was free to listen to what Leo was saying. Not that she could understand it, because he was talking in Italian, but it was lovely to listen to him anyway.

She always thought of him as English, like his mother, but then this amazing other side of him would come out, the Italian side that came from his father, and it did funny things to her insides.

Or maybe it was just the language doing that? That must be it. There was no way Leo talking Italian was sexy, that was just ridiculous. Not according to his numerous female fans, of course, but that didn't mean *she* had to fall under his spell. This was Leo, after all.

Yes, of course he was gorgeous, she knew that, and she'd had a serious case of hero-worship when she'd hit puberty, but she'd never felt whatever it was they all obviously felt—probably because she'd known him too long, knew all his weaknesses and irritating little habits as well as his strong points, like friendship and loyalty and generosity.

He was virtually a brother, a brother she loved to bits and would go to the end of the earth for. The best friend a girl could want. And no matter where she ended up, that would never change, but sexy? Nope—

'*Ciao. A dopo,*' he said in that delicious Italian of his, and her heart did a little back-flip to prove her wrong.

He put his phone away and smiled at Amy across the aisle.

'Well, that's our accommodation sorted,' he said with relief. 'I phoned Massimo Valtieri to tell him I'm bringing a friend to help with the baby so we'd make our own arrangements, but he wouldn't have any of it. He says there's plenty of room for you, too, and they're fine with us all staying at the *palazzo,* as from tonight. Problem solved.'

'*Palazzo*?' she squealed, and lowered her voice to a whisper. 'They live in a *palazzo?*'

Leo laughed softly at the awed expression on her face. 'Apparently. It's an old Medici villa. I've seen pictures of it, and it's very beautiful. It's been in the family for centuries, which is why I want to deal with them because it's not just a business, it's in their blood, it's who they are. The meetings will be there and they all live very close by, apparently, so it makes sense us being there, too, so if Ella kicks off and you can't cope, I won't be far away. And his wife's there, so you'll have company.'

'Oh, that's good,' she said, and a little worried crinkle in between her eyebrows smoothed away. She shook her head, her mouth kicking up in a wry smile. 'I still can't quite believe I'm going to be staying in a *palazzo*.'

She looked so flummoxed it made him chuckle. 'Well, you've got about four or five hours to get used to the idea,' he told her.

He was just relieved he'd be on hand; he didn't know what she knew about babies, but she knew almost nothing about Ella, so having a woman around who was a mother herself could only be a good thing, especially under the circumstances. He didn't want Amy feeling any more overwhelmed than she already was.

She was leaning over now and chatting to Ella, telling her what a lucky girl she was to stay in a *palazzo,* and he settled back in the seat and studied her. She was smiling, the haunted look in her eyes retreating as she fell under the spell of his tiny daughter, and for the briefest of fleeting seconds he wondered what life would have been like for all of them if she'd been Ella's mother.

It took his breath away.

CHAPTER THREE

AMY GLANCED ACROSS at Leo and frowned.

He was staring at her with the strangest expression on his face. 'Have I got a smut on my nose or something?'

'What? No. Sorry, I was miles away. Ah, here's Julie, we might be in business,' he added, and he sounded relieved, for some reason.

'We're about to take off now,' Julie said. 'Is there anything you need to ask before we're airborne?'

'I'm fine. Amy?' Leo said, raising an eyebrow at her.

'No, I'm fine, thank you.'

Julie left them, took herself off to her seat behind the cockpit, and then the pilot's voice came over the loudspeaker and they were off.

Leo strapped himself in, reached across with Ella's bottle and began to feed her as they turned at the end of the runway.

'It helps her ears to adjust to the pressure

change,' he explained, but Amy didn't care right then. She leant back, gripped the armrests and closed her eyes. She hated this bit—

'Oh!' She gasped as she was forced back into the seat and the plane tipped up and catapulted itself into the sky.

'Bit quicker off the ground than a heavy commercial jet,' Leo said with a grin as they levelled out and settled into a gentle climb, banking out over the Thames estuary and towards the coast.

She looked away from him, staring blindly out of the window at the slightly tilted horizon as the reality of what she'd done kicked in. They were still climbing—climbing up, up and away from England. Away from the wedding that hadn't been, the redundant marquee on the lawn next door, the dress lying in a crumpled heap on her bedroom floor.

And she was going to Italy. Not on her honeymoon, but with Leo and Ella. Without a husband, without a wedding ring, without the engagement ring that was sitting on her dressing table at home where she'd left it.

She looked down at her hand. Nope, no ring. Just a faint, pale line where it had been.

Just to check, she ran her finger lightly over the empty space on her finger, and Leo reached out to her across the aisle, squeezing her hand.

'You OK?' he murmured, as if he could read her mind.

She flashed him a smile but it felt false, forced, and she looked away again. 'Just checking it's not a dream. It feels like I'm on drugs. Some weird, hallucinogenic stuff.'

'No drugs. No dream. You're just taking time to get used to it. It's a bit of a shock, such a drastic change of course.'

Shock? Probably. Drastic, certainly. It felt like she was falling, and she wasn't sure if the parachute would work. She met his eyes, worrying her lip with her teeth. 'I wish I'd been able to get hold of Nick. He wasn't answering his phone.'

'Did you leave a message?'

She shook her head. 'I didn't really know what to say. "Sorry I dumped you at the altar in front of all our family and friends" seems a bit inadequate, somehow.'

'He didn't look upset, Amy,' Leo reminded her softly. 'He looked relieved.'

'Yes, he did,' she agreed. 'Well, I guess he would do, wouldn't he, not being stuck with me?'

Leo frowned. 'Why should he be relieved about that?'

'Because clearly I'm an idiot!'

Leo laughed softly, his eyes full of teasing affection. 'You're not an idiot,' he said warmly. 'Well, not much. You just got swept along by the momentum. It's easily done.'

It was. And he was right, she had. They both had. Was that what had happened to Leo and Lisa when he'd done the decent thing and married her for the wrong reasons?

The seatbelt light went off with a little ping, and Leo undid his lap strap and swung his seat round slightly as Julie approached them with a smile.

'Fancy a drink, Amy?' Leo asked her. 'Something to eat?'

Amy laughed. 'Eat? I couldn't eat another thing! That picnic was absolutely amazing. I'm still stuffed.'

'Well, let's just hope everyone enjoyed it. I'll have a cappuccino, Julie, please. Amy?'

'That would be lovely, thank you.'

Julie smiled and nodded, disappeared to the galley area behind the cockpit and left Amy to her thoughts. They weren't comfortable. All those people who'd travelled miles to see her married, and here she was running away with Leo and leaving them all in the lurch when she should have been there apologising to them.

'I wonder if they're all still there having a post-mortem on the death of my common sense?' she murmured absently. 'At least a lot of them turned up to eat the food. It would have been a shame to waste it.'

'I imagine most of them will have left by now—and your common sense didn't die, it just woke up a bit late in the day.'

'Maybe.' She sighed, and smiled at him ruefully. 'The food really was amazing, you know. I'm glad I got to try it. Do you know how long it is since you cooked for me?' she added wistfully, and he gave a soft huff of laughter.

'Years.'

'It is. At least four. Five, probably. You did it a lot when my father died. I used to come and hang out in your restaurant while I was at uni and you'd throw something together for us when you'd finished, or test a recipe out on me. I've missed that.'

'Me, too. I'm sorry. My life's been a bit chaotic since the television series.'

Well, that was the understatement of the century. 'So I gather,' she said mildly. 'And you've opened the new restaurant. That can't have been easy with a new wife and a baby on the way.'

A shadow flitted through his eyes and he looked away, his smile suddenly strained. 'No. It took a lot of my time. Too much.'

So much that their marriage had fallen apart? If they'd even had a marriage in the real sense. It didn't sound like it, but she knew very little more than he'd just told her and the rest was rumours in the gutter press. They'd had a field day, but his parents didn't talk about it, and until today she'd hardly seen Leo since before his marriage.

All she knew was what had been in the paper, that Lisa had been knocked down by a car late one stormy night and had died of her injuries, and the coroner had returned a verdict of accidental death. Ella had been tiny—two months old? Maybe not even that. And Leo had been left with a motherless baby, a new business venture that demanded his attention and a television contract he'd had to put on hold. Small wonder she hadn't seen him.

'Your cappuccino, Miss Driver.'

The drink was set down in front of her, and she flashed a distracted smile at Julie and picked up her spoon, chasing the sprinkled chocolate flakes around in the froth absently.

His hand came out and rested lightly on her arm, stilling it. 'It'll be all right, Amy,' he murmured, which made her smile. Trust Leo to be concerned for her when actually she was worrying about him.

'I'm fine,' she assured him. And she was, she realised. A little stunned, a little bemused almost at the turn of events, but Leo was whisking her away from it all so fast she didn't have time to dwell on it, and that could only be a good thing.

She pulled out her little pocket camera and pointed it at him. 'Smile for the birdie!'

'Make sure you get my good side.'

She lowered the camera and cocked an eyebrow at him. 'You *have* a good side?'

He rolled his eyes, that lazy grin kicking up his mouth and dimpling his right cheek, and her heart turned over. She clicked the button, turned to get an interior shot while her heart settled, and clicked again.

'Day one of your Tuscan tour blog,' she said lightly, and he laughed.

She caught it, grinned at him and put the camera away.

* * *

They landed shortly before five o'clock, and by five thirty they'd picked up the hire car and were on their way to the *palazzo*. Ella was whingeing a little, so he pulled over in a roadside *caffè* and ordered them coffee and pastries while he fed her from a pouch of pureed baby food.

It galled him to do it, but it wouldn't kill her. It was organic, nutritionally balanced, and had the massive advantage that it was easy. He had enough fish to fry at the moment without worrying about Ella.

He glanced up and met Amy's eyes. She was watching him, a strange expression on her face, and he tipped his head questioningly.

'What?'

'Nothing. Just—I've never really got used to the thought of you as a father, but you seem very comfortable with her.'

He looked back at Ella, his heart filling with love. 'I am. I didn't know what it would be like, but I love it—love her, more than I could ever have imagined loving anyone. She's the most precious thing that's ever happened to me.'

Amy's smile grew wistful. 'It shows,' she murmured, and he thought of all the plans she'd mentioned that she'd walked away from, all the things she'd sacrificed. Like starting a family. And if he hadn't interfered…

She might have ended up in the same mess as him, he reminded himself, bringing up a child on her own after the disastrous end of a doomed relationship.

'Amy, it'll happen for you, when the time's right,' he told her softly, and she gave a wry little smile that twisted his heart.

'I know. But I have to warn you, I don't know anything about babies so it won't hurt to practise on Ella so I can make my mistakes first with someone else's child.'

He chuckled, ruffling Ella's dark curls gently. 'You won't make mistakes, and even if you do, you won't break her. She's pretty resilient.'

Her wry smile turned to a grimace. 'That's probably just as well. She might need to be.'

'Chill, Amy. She's just a little person. She'll let you know what she needs.'

'Yeah, if you can mind-read a ten-month-old baby,' she said drily, but the smile reached her eyes now and he let his breath out on a quiet sigh of relief. She'd been hanging by a thread ever since she'd turned her back on Nick, and it had taken till now before he'd felt absolutely sure that she'd done the right thing. Having a baby with the wrong person was a disaster, and that's what she could have done if everything had gone to plan.

Which let him off the hook a bit on the guilt front.

'Here, you can start practising now. Give her the rest of this so I can drink my coffee, could you, please?' he asked, handing her the pouch and spoon and sitting back to watch. Amy took it cautiously, offered it to Ella, and the baby obediently sucked the gloop from the spoon, to Amy's delight and his relief. Contrary to her predictions, they seemed to be getting on fine. 'There—see?' he said lightly. 'Easy.'

She threw him a cheeky grin and put the empty pouch down. 'Well, this end was easy, but I think she'll need her daddy for the other one. I can only master one skill at a time and there'll be plenty of time to learn about that later.'

He laughed, put his cup down and scooped up Ella and the changing bag. 'I'm sure there'll be lots of opportunities.'

'I don't doubt it,' she said drily, but her wry, affectionate smile warmed his heart and he was suddenly fiercely glad that she'd come with them.

* * *

By the time the sun was getting low on the western horizon, they were turning onto the broad gravelled drive leading up to the Palazzo Valtieri.

The track dipped and wound along the valley floor, and then rose up the hill through an avenue of poplars to a group of stone buildings on the top, flushed rose by the setting sun.

'I think that's the *palazzo*,' he told her, and Amy felt her jaw drop.

'What, all of it? It's enormous! It looks as big as some of the little hilltop towns!'

He chuckled softly. 'There'll be all sorts of other buildings there clustered around it. It won't just be the house.'

But it was. Well, pretty much, she realised as they approached the imposing edifice with its soaring stone walls and windows that she just knew would have the most amazing views. She couldn't wait to get her proper camera out.

They drove under a huge stone archway in the wall and into a large gravelled courtyard, triggering lights that flooded the area with gold. There were several vehicles there, and Leo brought the car to rest beside a big people-carrier.

They were facing a broad flight of steps flanked

by olive trees in huge terracotta pots, and at the top of the steps was a pair of heavily studded wooden doors, totally in proportion to the building.

She felt her jaw sag again. 'Oh. Wow. Just—wow,' she breathed.

Leo's grin was wry. 'Yeah. Makes my house look a bit modest, doesn't it?'

'I haven't seen your house yet,' she reminded him, 'but it would have to be ridiculously impressive to compete with this.'

'Then it's a good job I'm not a sore loser. Unless you count a sea view? That's probably the only thing they don't have.'

She cocked her head on one side and grinned at him. 'That might just do it. You know me—I always wanted to be a mermaid.'

'I'd forgotten that.' His cheek creased, the dimple appearing as he punched the air. 'Ace. My house trumps the seat of the Valtieri dynasty.'

'I did say "might",' she pointed out, but she couldn't quite stifle her smile, and he laughed softly and opened the car door.

'You haven't seen my view yet.'

She met his smile over the top of the car. 'I

haven't seen theirs, either. Don't count your chickens.'

'Would I?' He grinned again, that dimple making another unscheduled appearance, and her heart lurched.

'I guess we'd better tell them we're here,' she said, but it seemed they didn't need to.

One of the great wooden doors swung open, and a tall man in jeans and a blinding white shirt ran down the steps, smiling broadly, hand extended as he reached Leo.

'Massimo Valtieri,' he said. 'And you're Leo Zacharelli. It's good to meet you. Welcome to Palazzo Valtieri.'

He spoke in perfect English, to Amy's relief, faintly accented but absolutely fluent, and he turned to her with a welcoming smile. 'And you must be Miss Driver.'

'Amy, please,' she said, and he smiled again and shook her hand, his fingers warm and firm and capable.

'Amy. Welcome. My wife Lydia's so looking forward to meeting you both. She's just putting the children to bed and the others are in the kitchen. Come on in, let me show you to your rooms so you can settle the baby and freshen up before you meet them.'

Leo took Ella out of the car seat and picked up the changing bag, Massimo picked up Leo's bag and removed hers firmly from her grip, and they followed him up the steps and in through the great heavy door into a cloistered courtyard. The sheltered walls were decorated with intricate, faded murals that looked incredibly old, and more olive trees in huge pots were stationed at the corners of the open central area.

It was beautiful. Simple, almost monastic, but exquisite. And she couldn't wait to start capturing the images. She was already framing the shots in her mind, and most of them had Leo in them. For his blog, of course.

Their host led them around the walkway under the cloisters and through a door into a spacious, airy sitting room, simply but comfortably furnished, with French doors opening out onto a terrace. The sun had dipped below the horizon now, blurring the detail in the valley stretched out below them, but Amy was fairly sure the view would be amazing. Everything else about the place seemed to be, and she just knew it would be crammed with wonderful photo opportunities.

Massimo pushed open a couple of doors to reveal two generous bedrooms, both of them opening out onto the same terrace and sharing a well-equipped bathroom. There was a small kitchen area off the sitting room, as well, and for their purposes it couldn't have been better.

'If there's anything else you want, please ask, and Lydia said she hopes you're hungry. She's been cooking up a storm ever since you rang and we'd love you to join us once you've got the baby settled.'

'That would be great, but she shouldn't have gone to any trouble. We don't want to impose,' Leo said, but Massimo was having none of it.

'No way! She's a chef, too, and not offering you food would be an unforgivable sin,' he said with a laugh. 'Just as soon as the baby's settled, give me a call on my mobile and I'll come and get you. Both of my brothers and their wives are here as well tonight. And we don't in any way dress for dinner, so don't feel you have to change. We'll be eating in the kitchen as usual.'

The door closed behind him, and Leo turned to her with a faintly bemused smile.

'Are you OK with this? Because I'm well aware you've had a hell of a day and I don't want to push it, but it does sound as if they want to meet us, or me, at least. If you don't feel up to company, just say so and I'll bring something over to you and you can have a quiet evening on your own. Up to you.'

Her stomach rumbled, answering the question, and she smiled ruefully. 'Honestly? Yes, I'm tired, but I'm absolutely starving, too, and I'm not sure I want to spend the evening on my own. And anyway, as you say, it's you they all want to meet. I won't understand what you're all saying anyway, so I'll just sit in the corner and stuff myself and watch you all.'

'I think you will understand, at least some of it. His wife's English.'

'Really?' Another knot of tension slid away, and this time her smile felt a bit more spontaneous. 'That's good news. I might have someone to talk to while you're in meetings.'

Leo chuckled. 'I'm sure you will. I'll just bath Ella quickly and give her a bottle and pop her into bed, and then we can go and meet the rest of the family.'

Ella! She hadn't even given her duties a thought, but now she did. 'Will it be all right to leave her, or do you want me to stay with her? It's you they want to meet.'

He picked something up off a side table and waggled it at her.

'Baby monitor,' he said, by way of explanation. 'They really have thought of everything.'

They had. Absolutely everything. There were posh toiletries in the bathroom, the fridge was stocked with milk, juice, butter and fresh fruit, there was a bowl of brown, speckled eggs and a loaf of delicious-looking crunchy bread on the side, and a new packet of ground coffee next to a cafetière. And teabags. Amy was glad to see the teabags. Real English ones.

While Leo heated the baby's bottle and gave it to her, she made them both a cup of tea and curled up on the sofa to wait for him. Ella fussed a little as he was trying to put her down, but it didn't take long before she went quiet, and she heard a door close softly and Leo appeared.

'Is that for me?' he asked, tilting his head towards the mug on the table in front of her.

She nodded. 'I didn't know how long you were going to be, so it might be a bit cold. Would you like me to make you a fresh one?'

'No, it's fine, I'll drink it now. Thanks. I ought

to ring Massimo anyway. I don't want to keep them waiting and Ella's gone out like a light.'

'Before you call him—did you say anything to them? About me, I mean? About the wedding?'

A frown flashed across his face. 'No, Amy, of course not. I didn't think you'd want to talk about it and it just puts an elephant in the room.'

'So—no elephants waiting for me?'

He gave a quiet grunt of laughter, the frown morphing into a sympathetic smile. 'No elephants, I promise.'

'Good,' she said, smiling back as the last knot of tension drained away, 'because I'm really, really hungry now!'

'When aren't you?' he muttered with a teasing grin, pulling out his phone, and moments later Massimo appeared and led them across the courtyard and into a bustling kitchen filled with laughter.

There were five people in there, two men and three women, all seated at a huge table with the exception of a pregnant woman—Lydia?—who was standing at the stove, brandishing a wooden spoon as she spoke.

Everyone stopped talking and turned to look at them expectantly, the men getting to their feet to greet them as Massimo made a quick round of introductions, ending with his wife. She'd abandoned her cooking, the wooden spoon quickly dumped on the worktop as she came towards them, hands outstretched in welcome.

'Oh, I'm so glad you've both decided to come over and join us. I hope you're hungry?'

'Absolutely! It smells so amazing in here,' she said with a laugh, and then was astonished when Lydia hugged her.

'Oh, bless you, I love compliments. And you're Leo,' she said, letting go of Amy and hugging him, too. 'I can't tell you how pleased I am to meet you. You've been my hero for years!'

To Amy's surprise, Leo coloured slightly and gave a soft, self-effacing chuckle. 'Thank you. That's a real compliment, coming from another chef.'

'Yeah, well, there are chefs and chefs!' Lydia said with a laugh. 'Darling, get them a glass of wine. I'm sure they're ready for it. Travelling with a baby is a nightmare.'

'I'm on it. Red or white?'

Leo chuckled and glanced over at Lydia. 'Judging by the gorgeous smell, I'd say a nice robust red?'

'Perfect with it. And it's one of your recipes,'

Lydia told him with a wry grin. 'I've adapted it to showcase some of our ingredients, so I hope I've done them justice.'

They launched into chef mode, and Amy found a glass of iced water put in her hand by one of the other two women. It appeared she was also English and her smile was friendly and welcoming.

'I don't know about you, but travelling always makes me thirsty,' she said. 'I'm Isabelle, and I'm married to Luca. He's a doctor, so more of a sleeping partner in the business, really. And this is Anita, the only native Valtieri wife. She's married to Giovanni. He's a lawyer and he keeps us all on the straight and narrow.'

'Well, he tries,' Anita said, her laughing words heavily accented, and Amy found herself hugged again. 'Welcome to Tuscany. Have you had a good day so far? I thought Leo was supposed to be at a wedding today, but obviously not.'

Well, how on earth was she supposed to answer that? Except she didn't have to, because Leo appeared at her side and answered for her, fielding the question neatly.

'We managed to get away early,' he said, and she only just stifled a laugh. 'The journey was great, though. Seamless. And our accommodation is perfect. Thank you all so much. It'll make it very much easier for all three of us.'

'You're welcome,' Massimo said, glasses and a bottle in hand, and he and his two brothers immediately engaged Leo in a conversation about the wine, so Amy turned back to the women and found herself seated at the table while they poured her a glass of wine and chatted about the business and the area and their children, and asked about Leo.

'So, how long have you known him?' Lydia asked, perching on the chair next to Amy in a break in her cooking.

'Oh—for ever. Our families have been neighbours since before I was born.'

'Gosh. Literally for ever! Lucky you!'

She laughed. 'I don't know about that. He used to test recipes on me when we were kids, but I was a willing victim.'

'Victim?'

She wrinkled her nose. 'He was a little adventurous, so there were a few interesting disasters along the way. I think his palate's refined a little bit since then.'

They all laughed, even Leo, and she realised

he'd been standing right behind her, listening to every word.

'Damned by faint praise,' he said wryly, and she swivelled round and looked up at him with a grin.

'Well, I wouldn't like to swell your head.'

'God forbid.'

His mouth twitched, and she laughed and turned back and found Lydia, Anita and Isabelle watching her thoughtfully. Why? They'd always behaved in this playful way, she just hadn't thought about it, but—were the three women reading something else into it? Something that wasn't there? She felt herself colour slightly and dunked a bit of olive ciabatta into the bowl of oil and balsamic vinegar on the table in front of her.

Good move. The flavour exploded on her tongue and suddenly she understood why they were there. 'Wow. This is lovely. Is it yours?' she asked, and to her relief the conversation moved on as the food was put on the table and they all piled in, and the slightly awkward moment passed.

Then as the last plate was cleared away and it looked as if they'd split up into two groups again, Ella cried out, the monitor flashing right in front of Leo, and Amy seized the opportunity to escape before the women could ask any more searching questions.

'I'll go,' she said hastily to Leo, scraping back her chair and snatching up the baby monitor. 'You stay and talk.'

'Are you sure?'

His eyes searched hers, concern etched in them, and she found a smile.

'Absolutely. We'll be fine, and if we aren't, we'll come and find you.' She turned to the others. 'I hope you'll excuse me. It's been quite a…long and complicated day.'

'Of course. We'll see you tomorrow. If there's anything you need, just ask,' Lydia said, and she nodded.

'Thanks.'

Leo reached out a hand and stopped her briefly. 'I'll be with you in a minute. I won't be long.'

She nodded back, dug out the smile again for the others, thanked Lydia for the meal and made her escape. Long and complicated didn't even begin to scratch the surface of her day, and she was only too ready to head across the beautiful courtyard to their suite of rooms, let herself in and close the door with a shaky sigh of relief.

For some reason she could feel tears threatening, and frankly she'd done enough crying this morning—no, this afternoon. Whenever. The wedding was supposed to have been at noon. So still less than twelve hours since she'd turned her back on Nick and run away.

And she would be spending her wedding night alone in an ancient medieval *palazzo* in Tuscany, instead of with Nick in the honeymoon suite of an old manor house prior to heading off to a sun-soaked beach in the Indian Ocean for her honeymoon.

She gave a tiny laugh that turned into a hiccupping sob, and ramming her hand over her mouth she headed towards the bedrooms.

And stopped, registering for the first time that the room with the travel cot in it had twin beds, and the other room had a huge double. Not that the twin beds were in any way small, but it seemed wrong for her to take the double instead of Leo and she was, after all, supposed to be here to look after the baby, even though Leo had said he'd share with Ella.

She pushed the door open a little further and peered into the travel cot. The baby was fast asleep and breathing quietly and evenly, whatever had disturbed her clearly not enough to wake her properly, and Amy turned away from the bedrooms and headed for the kitchen.

She was tired beyond belief, her brain worn out from going over and over the repercussions of her impulsive behaviour, but she couldn't go to bed until she'd discussed their sleeping arrangements with Leo, so she put the kettle on, made herself a cup of tea and settled down to wait for him.

CHAPTER FOUR

LEO STAYED IN the kitchen for a while longer, deep in conversation with the Valtieri brothers. They were fascinating men, with a passion for what they produced, for the land, for their family ties and history and also for their future—a future he realised he wanted to share.

Their business was a part of them, utterly fundamental, their enthusiasm burning so intensely that it was infectious. It was how he felt about his own chosen path, his constant striving for perfection, for excellence, and it was wonderful to meet people who produced the raw ingredients of his craft with the same passion.

He'd missed this—missed talking to people who understood what drove him and shared it, missed immersing himself in the thing he loved most in the world apart from his family. Especially his daughter—

His gut clenched. Oh, hell. Amy was looking after her, and he'd totally forgotten!

What was he thinking about? He'd let her take the baby monitor so he had no idea how long it had taken Ella to settle, and Amy had enough to deal with tonight, of all nights, without a tired and fractious baby.

He shouldn't have taken her for granted, but he'd been so wrapped up in his own agenda, so busy enjoying himself, that she'd completely slipped his mind.

How *could* he have let that happen? Especially when he was so worried about her. She'd been quiet all day, so unlike her usually bubbly self, and although she seemed to have enjoyed the evening there'd been a distracted look in her eyes—and when Ella had cried, she'd grabbed the opportunity to escape with both hands.

And he'd let her do it. What kind of a friend was he?

'Sorry, guys, I lost track of the time, I'm going to have to go,' he said a little abruptly. 'It's been a long day and I need to check on Ella.' And Amy. *Dio*, how *could* he—?

'Sure. We'll see you in the morning. Nine o'clock?'

He nodded. 'That's fine. I'll look forward to it.'

'Tell Amy we'll be around,' Lydia chipped in

with a smile. 'She and Ella are more than welcome to join us.'

'Thank you. I'll pass it on. I'm sure she'll appreciate the company. And thank you for a lovely meal. It was delicious. I'll have to return the favour one evening.'

Lydia laughed. 'Feel free. I'd love you to cook for us. It would be amazing. You can give me a master class, if you like.'

He gave a soft chuckle. 'No pressure, then.'

'I'm sure you can handle it, Chef,' she said with a grin, and he chuckled again and got to his feet, shook hands with all the men, said goodnight to the ladies and crossed the courtyard swiftly, letting himself quietly into the guest suite.

Silence. No screaming baby, no sound from Amy desperately trying to pacify her, and the tension drained out of him. She must have gone to bed and left a lamp on in the sitting room for him.

He turned towards it, and then he saw her in the soft glow, curled up in the far corner of a sofa, her hands cradling a mug and her face in shadow.

'You're still up,' he said unnecessarily. 'I'm sorry, I didn't mean to be so long. I take it Ella's OK?'

'She's fine.'

He frowned. Her voice sounded—odd. Disconnected.

'Amy?' he said softly. She turned her head and looked up at him, and his gut clenched. She'd been crying. He could see the dried tracks of tears on her cheeks, her eyes red-rimmed and swollen, and guilt rose up and swamped him.

Damn.

She hadn't meant him to find her like this, and now there was guilt written all over his face. She closed her eyes, biting her lip and kicking herself for not just going to bed.

The sofa dipped as he sat down next to her, his thigh warm against her hip, his arm around her shoulders solid and comforting. She felt his breath ease out on a weary sigh.

'I'm so sorry. I got caught up in conversation and I should have been here for you, not abandoning you on your own to deal with Ella. Was she a nightmare?'

She shook her head. 'No. She was still asleep. It's not that. I spoke to Nick,' she said, and her voice clogged with tears. She swallowed and tried again. 'He rang to find out if I was OK.'

'And are you?' he asked, although she knew he could see quite clearly that she wasn't.

She shrugged. 'I suppose. I don't know. It's my wedding night, Leo. I should have been married—'

Her voice cracked, and he took the mug out of her hands and pulled her gently into his arms.

'Oh, Amy, I'm so sorry. This is all my fault.'

'What's your fault?' she asked, tilting her head back and searching his eyes. 'That I left it so long to realise it was a mistake? Hardly.'

'That you're not married. Not on your honeymoon. That you've thrown away all your carefully laid plans.'

She shook her head and cradled his cheek in her hand. It felt rough, the stubble growing out now at the end of the day, and there was something grounding about the feel of it against her palm. Something warm and real and alive that made it all make sense. Or complicated it all a whole lot more. She dropped her hand back in her lap.

'That I'm not married to the wrong man,' she corrected, her voice soft but emphatic, needing to convince him so he didn't carry this guilt around like a burden for ever. 'You did the *right thing*, Leo. It was me who didn't, me who ignored all the warnings going off in my head all the time. I thought I was just stressing about the wedding, but I wasn't, it was the marriage, the lifetime commitment to him that was worrying me. I just didn't realise it. So for goodness' sake don't beat yourself up over it, because it's *not your fault*, OK?'

'So why are you crying?'

She gave a little shrug. 'Because the pressure's off? Because I feel guilty because I'm glad I'm not married to him when he's actually a really nice guy? Take your pick.' She tried to smile, but it was a rubbish effort, so she sniffed and swiped the tears off her cheeks and tried again. 'There. Is that better?'

'Not much,' he said honestly, lifting a damp strand of hair away from her eyes with gentle fingers.

'Well, it's the best I can do,' she said, her voice choked again, and Leo closed his eyes and folded her close against his chest and rested his cheek against her hair. It felt a little stiff from the products she must have had put in it for the updo, not as soft and sleek as usual. Not his Amy.

His Amy? What was he thinking? She hadn't ever been *his* Amy, even in the old days. And now was not the time to reinvent their relationship, when both of them were an emotional mess. However appealing it might be. And where the hell had that come from?

With a quiet sigh he loosened his hold and sat up a little, putting some much-needed distance between them before he did something stupid that he'd regret for ever.

'You'll feel better after you've had a good night's sleep. Why don't you have a shower and go to bed?' he murmured, and she looked up at him, her eyes lost.

'Where? Which bed? The room Ella's in has only got single beds and you can't possibly sleep in one of those, it seems all wrong. You should have the double.'

'Don't be daft. They're not small beds. You take the double, it's fine.'

'Are you sure?'

'Of course I'm sure, and I'm certainly not moving her tonight. I'll sort the luggage out, and then you go and have a shower and get off to bed. You'll feel better in the morning, honestly.'

'Is that a promise?'

She looked so forlorn that he laughed softly

and hugged her. 'Yes, it's a promise. New day, new life.'

It sounded great. He just hoped it didn't turn out to be a false promise, because he was still waiting for that new life after copious new days. New weeks. New months. And there was no sign of it. He felt as if his life was on hold, in limbo, and every dawn was just as bleak as the one before…

Leo was right. She did feel better in the morning.

It shouldn't have surprised her; Leo was always right. Why hadn't she asked him about Nick before? Except of course it would have seemed disloyal, and even now it felt wrong talking to him about Nick because there was nothing *wrong* with Nick.

It wasn't about Nick. It was about her, and the fact that it had taken her such an unforgivably long time to realise she wasn't going to settle for sensible.

She sighed softly. She'd never been sensible. She only had to look at the mess she'd made of her other relationships to know that, so she might have realised it was never going to work with Nick. Except that was the very reason she'd thought it *might* work, because for once it *was* sensible, and it had taken her far too long to realise she was wrong.

Well, at least she hadn't left it until after they were married. That would have been worse.

She threw back the covers and climbed out of the ridiculously enormous bed that Leo really should have had. She wished he *had* had it, because lying alone in the vast expanse of immaculate white linen had just underlined all the things she'd walked away from.

Still, as Leo had said, new day, new life. That was yesterday. Today was a new day, a fresh start, and she needed to get out there and embrace it.

'Bring it on,' she muttered, staring at herself in the mirror and digging out a smile. There. See? She could do it.

She could hear Leo and Ella in the little sitting room of their suite and they seemed to be having a lot of fun, babyish giggles interspersed with the deeper, soft rumble of Leo's voice. She'd go and join them, bask in the warmth of their love for each other and see if it could drive out this aching loneliness.

She delved in her suitcase for her dressing gown, and frowned. Damn. She'd completely forgotten that she hadn't brought the ratty old towelling thing that she'd had for a hundred years but a slippery little scrap of silk deliberately chosen because it was beautiful and elegant and undeniably sexy. To inject some fireworks into their honeymoon?

Maybe. It was what the garment was designed for, like the camisole nightdress she'd worn last night, and she hadn't even thought about it when she'd said that she was packed ready to go, but she should have done, she realised in dismay. Not that she'd exactly had a lot of time to think about it in the hurry to leave.

She contemplated getting dressed rather than going out into the sitting room what felt like half-naked, but she needed a cup of tea and a shower before she could put on her clothes, and it covered her from head to toe. She tugged the belt tighter and opened the door. There. Perfectly respectable, if a little on the thin side, and it was only Leo, after all.

Only?

Scratch that. He was dressed in a battered old T-shirt and jeans, his feet bare, and he was sitting cross-legged on the floor with Ella, playing peep-bo from behind a cushion and making her giggle hysterically. And for some ridiculous reason he looked as sexy as sin. It must be the bare feet, she thought, and dragged her eyes off them. Or the tug of the T-shirt across those broad, solid shoulders—

He's not sexy! She swallowed and wrapped her arms defensively around her waist. 'Hi, guys. Are you having fun?' she asked, smiling at Ella and trying to avoid Leo's eye as he turned to look at her over his shoulder.

'My daughter likes to see the sun rise,' he said drily, and she chuckled and risked another glance at him.

Mistake. His eyes were scanning her body and he looked quickly away, a touch of colour brushing the back of his neck, and she wished she'd just got dressed because now she'd embarrassed him. Oh, God. Did he think she was flaunting herself in front of him? Idiot! She should have dragged on her clothes and changed them after her shower—

'Tea?' he asked, in a perfectly normal voice that didn't for some reason sound quite normal because there was a tension vibrating in it that she'd never heard before.

'That'd be great. I'll make it.'

But he'd already uncoiled from the floor in one lithe movement and headed for the kitchen, as if he was suddenly desperate for some space between them. 'I've had two cups,' he said. 'I'll make yours, and you can sit and come round slowly and play with Ella while I have a shower, if that's OK. Deal?'

'Deal.'

He made it to the safety of the kitchen and let his breath out on a long, silent sigh of relief.

'Thank you,' she called after him.

'Don't mention it.'

He flicked the switch on the kettle, then stuck his head back round the corner while the kettle boiled, still managing to avoid her eyes by pretending to look at Ella. 'I've got a meeting at nine that'll probably go on all morning—will you be OK with her? She'll probably nap for a lot of it.'

'I'll be fine, I slept like a log. Were you OK in that single bed?' she asked.

Bed? Now she wanted to talk about the *bed*? He ducked back into the kitchen and busied himself with her mug, sending his unruly body a short, pithy reprimand. 'Fine, thanks,' he lied. 'I told you it would be.'

It hadn't been fine, but he wasn't telling her that. Oh, it had been perfectly comfortable, if he ignored the fact that he was used to sleeping in a huge bed all to himself. What wasn't fine was the fact that he'd been ridiculously conscious of her just on the other side of the wall, and swapping rooms wouldn't change that. It would also mean sleeping in her sheets, and he'd had enough trouble getting her out of his thoughts as it was, without lying there surrounded by the haunting scent of her.

He made her tea and went back through just as she was trying to rearrange the dressing gown over her legs on the floor, and he put the tea down out of Ella's reach and went on walking, keeping his eyes firmly off the slim, shapely thigh barely concealed by that slippery scrap of silk that wouldn't stay where it was put.

'Back in a minute. Don't forget to drink it while it's hot.'

He closed the bathroom door with a frustrated sigh and shook his head. Where the hell had this crazy attraction come from? Not that she was helping, flitting about in that insubstantial little silk thing, but why should that affect him now? It never had before, and Amy frankly wasn't his type.

He liked sophisticated women, and there had

been plenty to choose from, especially since the first television series. But he'd used discretion, or so he'd liked to think, until Lisa. Nothing discreet or sophisticated about that. They'd brought out the worst in each other, and the only good thing to come of it was Ella. Their entire relationship had been a disaster of epic proportions, and Lisa had paid for it with her life. He'd never forgive himself for that, and there was no way he was ready for another relationship, especially not one with someone as vulnerable and emotionally fragile as Amy.

Sure, she was a woman now, a beautiful, warm, caring woman, and without a shadow of doubt if she'd been anybody else he wouldn't have hesitated. But she wasn't, she was Amy, and she trusted him. It had taken a huge amount of courage to call a halt to her wedding the way she had, and she'd turned to him for help. The last thing he'd do was betray that trust.

However tempting she'd looked in that revealing bit of nonsense. Oh, well. Maybe Ella would be sick on it and she'd have to wear something else and everything would get back to normal.

He could only hope…

* * *

By the time she emerged from the shower, he'd had breakfast and was ready to leave.

'I have to go, I'm supposed to be meeting up with them at nine,' he said, fiddling with his phone. 'Are you sure you'll be all right? Lydia said they'll be around. They all stayed over last night so you should have some company.'

'Fine. Great. And of course I'll be all right,' she said, crossing her fingers behind her back. 'Just go. We're fine, aren't we, Ella?'

He flicked her a quick glance, nodded, kissed Ella goodbye, handed her to Amy and left.

Not popular. The baby gave a little wail, and it took all the skill Amy hadn't known she had to distract her from the loss of her beloved father.

'He'll be back soon,' she promised, and retrieved the dragonfly and squished it, making it crackle. It worked, thankfully, and she ended up sharing her toast with Ella before they went to find the others.

They were in the kitchen, the women chatting at the table while the younger children played on the floor and the two oldest, both girls, sat quietly reading at the table.

'Amy, hi,' Lydia said with a smile. 'Have you had breakfast?'

'Yes, thanks, we're done. Leo said I should come and find you, if that's OK?'

'Of course it's OK. Would you like a coffee?'

'Oh, that would be lovely, if you're having one. Thanks.'

'I'm not, but it's no problem to make you one. We're all on fruit teas—caffeine and pregnancy doesn't go well together,' she said with a wry smile. 'Black, white, latte, cappuccino?'

They were *all* pregnant?

'Um—cappuccino would be lovely. Thanks.'

'I'm sorry, I'll see you outside,' Isabelle said, getting to her feet with a grimace. 'I can't stand the smell of it.'

'No, don't let me drive you out, I'll have tea!' she protested, but Isabelle laughed.

'You're fine. It'll be OK outside and we were just going out there anyway. Max, Annamaria, come on.'

They all went, leaving Amy alone with Lydia while she made the coffee, and Amy took it with a rueful grimace.

'I really wouldn't have had one if I'd known. I feel so guilty.'

'Oh, don't,' Lydia said with a laugh. 'We're used to it, and the men still drink coffee. They just do it elsewhere. One of us always seems to be pregnant and they're well trained.'

That made her smile. She couldn't imagine anything making Leo give up coffee. 'So, is this your fifth baby, or have I lost count?' she asked as they headed for the doors.

'Gosh, no! It's only my second. Massimo was widowed just after Antonino was born,' she explained, 'and I didn't know when we met if he'd want any more, but he just loves children, so this is our second, which will be his fifth, and Anita's on her second, and it's Isabelle's third—her husband's an obstetrician, which is quite handy.'

'Keeping it in the family?'

She chuckled. 'Something like that,' she said and led Amy outside onto the terrace. It seemed to wrap all around the outside of the house, giving stunning views over the surrounding countryside, and Amy was blown away by it.

They settled in the shade of a pergola draped with sweetly scented jasmine, and she cradled her cup and stared out over the beautiful valley below them, taking the time to soak up the scents and sounds that drifted around them on the air.

'Gosh, it's so beautiful here, I could take a lot of this,' she murmured. 'And the *palazzo* is absolutely fabulous.'

'Not when you have to clean it,' Lydia said with a laugh, 'but at least we have some help. And, yes, of course it's beautiful. We all feel very privileged to be guardians of it for future generations.'

'Well, there'll be no shortage of them,' she said with a smile. 'Would you mind if I took some photos of it? Leo's asked me to take some for his blog while we're in Italy, and this would be fantastic. We'd let you vet them first, of course.'

'Of course we wouldn't mind,' Lydia said. 'I'm sure the guys would be thrilled if it appeared in his blog. Just make sure he gives us a plug!'

'Oh, I'm sure he will. I haven't seen him look as fired up and enthusiastic as this in ages. Not that I'm surprised. It's just amazing here.'

'It is,' Isabelle agreed softly. 'It's a wonderful place to live, and it really doesn't take very long to fly home, which is great for keeping in touch with our families. Well, you know how long it takes, you've just done it.'

'Yes, but it doesn't really count. Our trip was ridiculously easy because Leo wangled a private charter from City Airport—'

'No!' Lydia said, laughing. 'Really? That's where I met Massimo! I was in a truly awful wedding dress, trying to blag a flight to Italy for a runaway bride competition—'

Amy sucked in her breath sharply, and Lydia stopped and frowned at her, her expression appalled. 'Amy—what did I say?'

She laughed. She had to laugh, there was nothing else to do really under the circumstances apart from cry, and she'd done enough of that. Time to introduce the elephant.

She gave them a brief précis of her impulsive actions, and Isabelle reached out and rested a hand lightly on her arm, her eyes searching. 'Oh, Amy. Are you sure you're all right?'

'Yes, of course I am,' she said lightly. 'Or I will be once the dust has settled.'

'Much more all right than if you'd married the wrong man,' Anita put in wryly. 'I wish more people had the sense to pull out instead of making each other miserable and putting their children through hell.'

Just as she and Nick might have done. She felt sick, thinking how close she'd come to it, how devastating it would have been for all of them.

Then Ella toppled over trying to pull herself up,

which gave Amy the perfect excuse to leave the conversation for a moment and regroup. Not that the women had been anything other than kindness itself, but she just didn't want to talk about her not-quite wedding or their relentlessly burgeoning happy families. The full extent of what she'd turned her back on was still sinking in, but, although the shock was receding, in its place was a terrifying emptiness that she wasn't ready to explore.

Was Nick feeling the same sense of loss? Maybe. Or maybe not. He'd asked if she minded if he went on their honeymoon alone, and of course she'd said no, but she wondered now if it was a good idea for him or if it would just be making it worse.

Not that it could be much worse than her running full tilt down the aisle away from him. God, the humiliation!

She groaned quietly, and Lydia shot her a thoughtful look and got to her feet.

'I need to make lunch. Are you two staying or going?'

'We're going,' Isabelle said briskly, standing up too. 'Anita and I are going to plan a shopping trip for baby stuff.'

Anita frowned. 'We are?'

'Yes, you know we are. We talked about it the other day.'

Or not, Amy thought, because Anita looked confused for a micro-second and then collected herself, scooped up her baby and went, leaving Amy alone with Lydia.

Two down, one to go, she thought with relief, and Lydia had to make lunch, so she could excuse herself—

'Come and talk to me while I cook.'

'Ella could do with a nap,' she said hastily, using the now grizzling baby as an excuse to escape, but Lydia just shrugged.

'Put her down, then, and come back. Bring the baby monitor. She'll be fine.'

Of course she would, and she went down like a dream, so Amy had no justification for not going back to the kitchen and facing what she felt was going to be an inquisition.

It wasn't, of course. Lydia was far too sensible and sensitive to do something so crass, and her smile of welcome was just that. There was a jug of what looked like home-made lemonade in the middle of the table, alongside two glasses, and Lydia was sitting there chopping vegetables while her children played outside the doors.

'That was quick. She's a good baby, isn't she?' she said as Amy sat down. 'Have you had much to do with her, or is she just good with people?'

'She must be. I haven't really been around recently and nor has Leo, so I haven't seen either of them much. I've been busy planning the wedding and working in London, and since Leo's wife died…' She gave a little shrug. 'Well, he hasn't had a lot of time for anything but work and Ella,' she trailed off awkwardly.

Lydia slid a glass of lemonade towards her. 'Yes, I can imagine. It must have been awful for him, and it must be a nightmare juggling his work with Ella. I know what it's like running one restaurant, never mind a group like theirs, and raising a baby is a full-time job on its own. I'm surprised he hasn't got a nanny.'

'I don't think he needs one at the moment. His parents are close by and they've helped him a lot, but he likes to be hands on. Even so, I think it's been a real struggle.'

'It was good of you to offer to help him.'

She gave a little laugh that hitched in the middle. 'Well, I didn't have anything else to do, did I? And he didn't have to try hard to convince me.

I love Italy, and I owe him big time. He's done a lot for me over the years.'

Lydia's eyes searched her face for a second before she turned her attention back to the vegetables. 'Like making sure you didn't marry the wrong man?

Her smile felt a little twisted. 'Absolutely. That's probably the biggest single thing he's ever done for me. He was giving me away—or not,' she said, trying to laugh it off, but the laugh turned into a sigh. 'My father died eight years ago, just after I went to uni, and I suppose I could have asked my uncle or his father or someone, but I wanted Leo, because he knows me better than anyone else on the planet. So I'm really rather glad I did or I might have ended up married to Nick and it would have been a disaster. Not that there's anything wrong with Nick, he's a lovely guy, it's just…'

'You weren't right for each other?' Lydia said wryly, meeting her eyes again.

She returned the understanding smile. 'Pretty much. Although why it took me so long to work out I have no idea. Probably because there *is* nothing wrong with him!' She gave a wry chuckle.

'And it's nothing to do with you and Leo?' 'No! Absolutely not!' she protested. 'I've known him

all my life. It would be like marrying my brother.'
Except it hadn't felt like that this morning, seeing him on the floor with Ella, when he hadn't been able to look at her, or her at him…

Lydia shrugged and gave a rueful smile. 'Sorry. It's not really any of my business, but—there just seems to be something, almost like some invisible connection, a natural rapport between you,' she said gently. 'Like with Anita and Gio. It took them years to work out what we could all see. And you seem to be so good together.'

Amy shrugged. 'He's just a really great friend. Or he was, but then Nick came along just after Leo's career took off, and then of course he got married, and Nick and I got engaged—and you know the rest. As I say, we've hardly seen each other recently, but he's still just Leo and I know if I ever need him I only have to ask. He's always got time for me, and he's still a really good friend. The sort you can lean on.'

Lydia nodded slowly. 'Well, I'm glad for you that you've got him. Going through something like this, you need a good friend to lean on. There's nothing like being with someone you don't have to explain yourself to, someone who knows you inside out and loves you anyway. I couldn't want a better friend than Massimo by my side.'

She threw the chopped vegetables in the pot, gave them a quick stir, put the lid on and turned back with a smile.

'So, tell me, what do you do when you're not running away from bridegrooms and being Leo's guinea pig?'

Amy laughed, as she was meant to, and the conversation moved on to safer, less turbulent waters, but Lydia's words echoed in Amy's head for the rest of the day.

Sure, she and Leo were the best of friends, but did that have to mean they couldn't be anything else to each other? Not now, of course. She was an emotional mess, and he was still dealing with the fallout of Lisa's death, but maybe, some time in the future…

…someone who knows you inside out and loves you anyway…

Like Leo?

And it suddenly occurred to her that for all these years, like Gio and Anita, they could have been missing something blindingly obvious that was right under their noses.

CHAPTER FIVE

THE MEN CAME back at lunchtime, and she found herself looking at Leo in a new light.

She could see just from the look on his face how much he'd enjoyed the morning, and their discussions continued for a few minutes, standing outside the kitchen door on the terrace with long, cold drinks in their hands, and they were all talking Italian.

It was the first time she'd heard them together like that, and it dawned on her with blinding clarity that, yes, it was a musical language but, no, they didn't *all* sound sexy. It wasn't the language, it was *Leo* talking the language.

Which changed everything.

They switched back to English as they came into the kitchen, but his voice still did things to her that no one else's did, and when he scooped Ella up in his arms and smiled the smile he reserved for her, Amy's heart melted all over again.

The conversation over lunch was very animated,

but that didn't stop him juggling little Ella on his lap while he ate, and after lunch he handed her back to Amy reluctantly.

'I'm sorry. We're going out again to look at the olive oil processing plant this afternoon, if that's OK? Has she been all right?'

He looked a little worried, but Amy just smiled and shook her head slowly. 'She's been fine, Leo. Just go and do what you want to do. We're OK here. Lydia's been looking after us, haven't you, Lydia?'

Lydia smiled reassuringly. 'Leo, don't worry about us. Amy and I are getting on like a house on fire, and Ella seems perfectly happy. Just go. Shoo. We're fine.'

He frowned fleetingly, then gave a brisk nod, kissed the baby and left with the others, and to her relief the baby didn't cry this time.

'Have you got swimming things with you?' Lydia asked as the door closed behind them. 'We've got a heated pool, just in case you were wondering.'

Amy frowned. 'Yes, I have, but I don't know if Ella has.'

Lydia flapped a hand. 'She doesn't need one. I've got loads of swim nappies and arm bands and things. She'll be fine, and it'll only be us and the kids,' she said with a smile, and Amy felt herself relax.

'It sounds lovely. Really inviting.'

Lydia laughed. 'Oh, it is. I think we'd die without it when it gets really hot. At the end of a scorching day in the summer, it's just gorgeous to sink under that water in the evening when the kids are in bed and the stars are glittering overhead. So romantic.' She grinned mischievously. 'You and Leo should try it one night.'

She laughed awkwardly. 'I think the romance might be rather lost on us,' she said, trying not to picture herself and Leo alone under the stars.

Lydia found her a swim nappy, and they all changed and made their way to the pool set down below the terrace at a lower level. The water felt blissful on her hot skin, and Ella seemed to love it, so they spent hours playing in the pool, and it was lovely.

Ella, finally exhausted by all the fun, got a little grizzly, so Amy gave her a bottle and put her down to sleep in a travel cot strategically situated in the shade. She went out like a light, leaving nothing for Amy to do except chill out.

She should have brought a book with her, but

she hadn't thought of it, so she settled herself on a sun lounger, arms wrapped round her knees, basking in the late afternoon sun and watching Lydia and the children playing in the water under the shade of a huge hanging parasol. Their squeals of delight washed over her as she gazed out over the beautiful valley below and soaked up the sun, and for the first time since the wedding that hadn't happened she felt herself relaxing.

Till the men appeared.

'The girls must be swimming,' Massimo said, and led Leo across the terrace to the railings. He could hear splashing and shrieking, and he leant on the railings beside Massimo and looked down at them.

Lydia was on the side with the youngest, wrapping him in a towel, and the other children were still in the water, but Amy was sitting on a sun lounger and he could see Ella sleeping in a travel cot in the shade just below them.

'Well, hi, there,' he said, and she looked up, her eyes shielded from him by her sunglasses.

'Hi,' she said, and wrapped her arms around her knees a little self-consciously. Not surprising. He could tell from here that her bikini was pretty insubstantial, and he felt himself willing her to unfurl her body so he could see it.

She smiled up at them, but it looked a little forced. Because of the bikini? Another honeymoon special, he thought, and his body cheered.

'Had a good time?' she asked, and he nodded.

'Great. Really interesting, but quite hot. That water looks very tempting.'

'Feel free, Leo. We've just finished,' Lydia said, gathering up the children's things and heading up the steps with the baby, the older children trailing in her wake, 'but help yourself. You're more than welcome to use it any time you like.'

'Yes, do,' Massimo agreed. 'I'd love to join you but I need to make a few calls before I can escape.' And taking the baby from her arms, he went inside with Lydia and the children, leaving Leo alone with Amy.

She didn't look any too thrilled. Because of the bikini? She would have worn it in public with Nick, he felt sure, so why did the fact that she was alone with him make any difference? Except of course it did. It certainly made a difference to him.

He went down the steps and crossed over to her, sitting on the edge of the sun lounger beside hers and pushing his sunglasses up onto his head so he could study her better. 'You've caught the sun,' he said with a slow smile. 'Just here.'

And because he couldn't resist it, he trailed a finger over her shoulder, and the heat that shot through him should have blistered his skin. Hers, too.

Why? It wasn't as if her skin was that hot. 'Mind if I join you for a swim?' he asked, and she shifted, straightening up so her shoulder was out of reach and giving him a perfect view of her cleavage.

'Actually, I'm going to go in, if you don't mind. I've been out here quite long enough,' she said, and swung away from him, getting to her feet on the other side of the sun lounger and wrapping the towel round herself quickly—but not before he'd been treated to the sight of her smoothly rounded bottom scarcely covered by a triangle of fabric, and his body reacted instantly.

She gathered up her things with indecent haste and turned to him, not quite meeting his eyes.

'Do you mind watching Ella till she wakes up? I could do with a shower.'

He swallowed. 'No, that's fine. How long's she been asleep?'

'I don't know. Half an hour? Bit more, maybe.

She was pooped after the swimming. She's had a bottle.'

He nodded. 'OK. You go ahead, I'll take care of her.'

She walked slowly up the steps and across the terrace, resisting the urge to run away. She had been doing a lot of that recently, and look where it had got her, but the heat in his eyes had stirred something inside her that she couldn't trust herself not to act on, and she couldn't get away from him quick enough.

Because it echoed what she felt for him? Or because she feared it was just the knee-jerk reaction of a healthy adult male to a woman in about three square inches of fabric? In which case doing anything other than retreating could just embarrass them both.

She went in through the kitchen, across the courtyard and into their suite, closing the door behind her with relief. She didn't know how long he'd be before he followed her, but she wasn't going to hang around.

She showered quickly, opened her suitcase to look for some after-sun lotion and found the sheet of contraceptive pills that were part of her morning routine. She lifted them out slowly, staring at them without seeing while all thoughts of Leo drained away.

It was to have been her last course before she and Nick started trying for a baby, and she felt an aching sense of loss that had nothing to do with Nick and everything to do with the unfulfilled promise of motherhood.

Ironic that she'd never had much to do with babies before, and yet here she was now, surrounded by pregnant women and small children, so that just when it was suddenly out of reach she saw exactly what she'd be missing.

She hesitated for a moment, then popped the now purposeless pill out of the sheet and swallowed it, simply because she didn't want her cycle messed up.

She found the after-sun lotion, smeared it on her shoulders where she could still feel the tingle of Leo's fingertip, pulled on clean clothes and emerged from the bedroom just as he appeared, Ella grizzling unhappily and arching backwards in his arms.

'She's a bit grumpy, aren't you, sweetheart?' Leo murmured gently, his voice rich with the warmth of his love. He looked up from the baby and smiled at Amy, and the vague sense of loss she'd been feeling was overlaid with another, much more complex emotion that was much more troubling.

'I don't suppose you fancy putting the kettle on, do you?' he suggested. 'I could murder a cup of tea.'

'It was my next job,' she said lightly, and walked past them into the kitchen, wondering how on earth, when her world was steadily imploding, the scent of Leo's skin warmed by the sun could possibly be so intoxicating...

The next morning Lydia dropped the children off at school and ran a few errands, so Amy followed her suggestion and spent a while exploring the grounds with the baby in the buggy, taking photos either for Leo or possibly her own portfolio. Assuming she could find an outlet for them, which was by no means certain. Still, just to be on the safe side, she kept clicking, and she took lots of photos of Ella for Leo.

He checked in on his mobile from time to time, just to make sure that everything was OK, and then Lydia collected the children from school and the men came home for lunch, and after that they all went in the pool to cool off before the men went back to work.

It was stiflingly hot, so Amy joined them, but it didn't take very many minutes to realise that frolicking about in the water in her skimpy little honeymoon bikini in front of Leo wasn't clever. It had been bad enough yesterday when she'd just had to stand up and wrap herself in a towel, but in the water everything seemed to take on a life of its own and she'd had an embarrassing wardrobe malfunction when Ella had grabbed her bikini top. It was only by a miracle that no one else had noticed, but Leo had, and she vowed never to do it again, no matter how tempting the water was.

Then Ella started to fuss, so she grabbed the opportunity and climbed out of the pool, swathed herself in her towel and took the baby from Leo in the water, towelling her gently dry and putting a nappy on her before giving her a drink and settling her in the travel cot for a nap.

Leo swam to the side and folded his arms on the edge of the pool. 'Coming back in?'

'No, I don't think so,' she said without looking at him. 'I thought I could take some photos of you all for the blog.'

'Sure?'

'Sure.'

She forced herself to meet his searching gaze, then he shrugged and sank back under the water, leaving her to it.

She stayed resolutely on the side, wrapped in her towel and perched on a sun lounger, and spent the next hour capturing images of them all playing in the water with the children—ostensibly for Leo, since a disproportionate number of the photos were of him, but mostly so she didn't have to frolic about feeling hopelessly under-dressed.

Then Ella woke, so Leo swam to the side and vaulted out, water streaming off his lean, muscular frame and plastering his shorts to strong, straight thighs, and her heart somersaulted in her chest. She clicked the shutter, capturing the image for posterity, then put the camera away in its case, giving him time to grab a towel and knot it loosely round his hips.

'Your turn to swim, I'll look after Ella,' he said, but she shook her head and glanced back at him.

Not better. Not better at all. To her all too vivid imagination it just looked as if he had nothing on under the towel, and it was too much for her.

'I'm going to shower and get dressed, and then I'll download the photos,' she said, getting hastily to her feet, and with a smile and a wave to the others, she picked up her camera and headed for the sanctuary of the house.

She hardly saw him on Tuesday because the men didn't come back for lunch and then had a meeting after dinner, but then on Wednesday afternoon Massimo and Gio had a prior commitment and the women and children were at a birthday party, so they were left to their own devices.

'How about playing tourists?' Leo suggested, so they went out in the car with the baby and explored a nearby hill town Lydia had recommended for its food shops, and while he investigated them she clicked away on her camera, recording the day for Leo's blog.

It made her smile, watching him interacting with the shopkeepers. He went all Italian, of course, smiling and laughing and waving his hands all over the place, and she realised that he was always like that when he was fired up about something, and she just hadn't registered it until now, when it was slightly more exaggerated.

He'd always been just Leo, and she'd never really analysed him before, but she was doing it now, constantly, with every click of the shutter.

Every move, every smile, every frown, every gesture, all logged and recorded in a little part of her brain labelled 'Leo', and her feelings were getting utterly confused.

Inappropriate? No, maybe not that, but certainly different, threatening the platonic status quo that she'd just realised was so fragile, and because of that, and because she wasn't going to repeat the fiasco with her bikini, when she spotted a likely-looking shop she took the opportunity to check it out.

'Can I have five minutes?' she asked him. 'I need another swimming costume if we're going to swim every day.'

A muscle twitched in his jaw and he nodded. 'Sure. I'll wait here for you.'

The shop was perfect, and she found a ludicrously expensive but utterly plain black one-piece swimsuit. She didn't bother to try it on. Whatever it was like, it had to be better than the bikini, and there was a limit to how many photos even she could take of Leo in and around the water. And anyway she wanted to swim; she just wasn't going to risk another disaster.

She picked up a pretty little pink swimsuit for Ella, as well, because it was irresistible, and she didn't even look at the price. She'd hardly given the baby anything, only the crackly dragonfly that was her constant companion, so she could easily justify it to herself.

She managed to pay without flinching, put her purse away, scooped up her shopping and went out into the sunshine to find Leo and Ella.

He wondered what she was looking for. Hopefully something that covered her up a little more successfully than that bikini, which had already given him two sleepless nights since Ella had grabbed it.

He was trying to keep an eye on the shop door, but an elderly matron who should have known better had cornered him and was flirting outrageously, so he was relieved to see Amy emerge.

'Got what you wanted?' he asked, and she nodded and waggled the bag at him.

'Yup. Are you done?'

'Definitely. We need to make a move.'

He turned to the woman to excuse himself, and she caught him by the shoulders and kissed his cheeks, laughing as she let him go with an outrageous parting shot and a cheeky pat on his behind.

He felt the colour run up his neck and walked hastily away, shaking his head in despair.

'What did she say to you?' Amy asked, eyeing him curiously as she struggled to keep up.

'Nothing,' he mumbled. 'Just goodbye.'

'I don't believe you. She was flirting—and she groped you.'

'No, she didn't. It was just a little pat. She recognised me, that's all.'

Amy rolled her eyes. 'I wasn't born yesterday, Leo. Most people don't pat you on the behind, and even I can tell a starstruck old biddy when I see one. She was hitting on you.'

He fought the rising tide of colour, and lost. 'OK, OK. She said if she was twenty years younger, she'd give you a run for your money. I didn't think it'd be wise to point out that we're not together. She might have dragged me off on her broomstick.'

Her chuckle was delicious, and he couldn't help but join in.

'You're such a babe magnet, Zacharelli,' she teased. 'They all hurl themselves at you, it doesn't matter how old they are.'

All except Amy.

The thought popped into his head without warning, but it was true. If he was such a babe magnet, how come she'd never even noticed him in that way? Well, not since she was fourteen and had come down with a serious case of hero-worship, and that didn't really count. Although God only knows he'd noticed *her* recently. Like Monday, with the bikini top that Ella had so helpfully dragged out of the way and that she'd now seen fit to replace. He'd certainly noticed that.

'Can we change the subject, please?' he muttered, to himself as much as Amy, and headed back to the car with Ella, leaving Amy to follow, still chuckling, in his wake.

The next day the men were out again, visiting the cousin who made the gorgeous balsamic vinegar that appeared with oil and bread at every delicious meal, and she and the three wives were left to their own devices for the whole day.

It seemed odd now, not seeing him at all for such a long time, and she seemed to miss him more than the baby did, which was a bit telling. They went to Isabelle's for lunch, for a change, and then retreated to the pool in the afternoon, and then at five, as they were just getting the children out of the water, Massimo, Gio and Leo reappeared, making her profoundly glad she'd bought the new one-piece.

Leo walked towards her, his eyes shielded by sunglasses, and she turned, the baby on her hip, to point him out.

'Hey, look, baby, it's your daddy!' she cooed to Ella, and Ella held her arms out to him, little starfish hands opening and closing as she jiggled with excitement.

Amy could identify with that. She watched Leo's face light up as he reached out for the baby, and felt a pang of envy. What would it be like, to have a little person so very pleased to see you?

Wonderful. Amazing.

He slid the sunglasses up onto his head and held his arms out, and she could see the wonder in his eyes.

'She's wet,' Amy warned him, but he just shrugged.

'I don't care. I need a shower anyway. Come here, *mia bellissima bambina*,' Leo said, reaching for the baby, but his fingers brushed Amy's breast and she sucked in her breath. It was barely audible, but he heard it, and their eyes clashed and held, his darkening to midnight.

For a moment they both froze. She couldn't breathe, the air jammed solid in her lungs, and then with a muttered apology he lifted Ella out of her arms and turned away, laughing and kissing her all over her face, making her giggle deliciously and freeing Amy from his spell.

After a second of paralysing immobility, she grabbed a towel and wrapped it firmly round herself, then gathered up their things and headed for the steps, Leo falling in beside her at the top. They walked back together to their apartment, Ella perched on his shoulders with her little fists knotted in his hair, while he told her a little about his day and they both pretended that the moment by the pool hadn't happened.

'Sounds like it was worth going,' she said lightly as they went in and closed the door behind them, and he nodded.

'It was,' he said, prising the baby's fingers out of his hair and swinging her down into his arms. 'We had a lot to talk about, and we still have. And they're all off to visit their parents tomorrow. It's their mother's birthday and they can't reschedule, there isn't another time they're all available, which means we can't finalise the deal until after they're back on Sunday. Will that be a problem for you?'

A whole weekend alone with Leo? She felt a flicker of trepidation—anticipation? She didn't know. All she knew was that she couldn't refuse him and she didn't want to. 'No—why should it?'

He shrugged. 'I don't know. I said maybe a week, but we won't leave now until at least Monday or Tuesday and I don't know if you can give me that long or if there's something you need to get back for.'

She stared at him blankly. 'Leo, I can give you as long as it takes. That's why I'm here. I owe you so much, for so many things—really, don't give it another thought. Do what you need to do. It's fine. I have nowhere else to be.'

'Sure?' he asked, but she could see the relief in his eyes and she wondered if he'd expected her to refuse.

She rolled her eyes. 'Of course I'm sure. Anyway, I'm having fun,' she said, keeping it light. 'So I'm going to be forced to spend a few more days in a medieval Medici palace with a beautiful swimming pool and a view to die for, playing with a cute baby and being fed by a celebrity chef. What a tragedy!'

He laughed softly, shrugged acknowledgement and put Ella on the floor on her towel, crouching down to peel off her costume. 'This is lovely, by the way. Really cute. Where did it come from? Did you borrow it?'

'No, I bought it yesterday in the shop while you were being chatted up by Methuselah's mother—and before you say anything, it's a present. So, are we going to be completely on our own, then, while they're away?' she asked, striving for casual while her hormones were having a field day.

'I believe so. They're going to give us keys and we'll have the run of the place till Sunday lunchtime, so we'll be able to just chill out, which is lovely. I really need that. It'll be like being on holiday, and I'll have a chance to try out some recipes using their ingredients. I'm actually really looking forward to it. I'm cooking for them all on Sunday so they don't have to do it when they get back, and I want to play around with some ideas for that.'

'Can I be your guinea pig?' she asked hopefully, latching onto the safe and familiar, and he tilted his head to look at her and grinned, suddenly looking like the old Leo.

'I'm relying on it. You have a terrifying gift for honesty where my food's concerned. And I'll try not to poison you.'

'You do that,' she said, secretly flattered by his backhanded compliment and relieved that the conversation had steered them seamlessly into safer waters.

'So how was your day?' he asked, straightening up with the naked baby in his arms. 'I felt I'd abandoned you. Were you both OK?'

'Leo, we were fine, and we've had a lovely day together. She's gorgeous. I didn't realise what fun a baby could be.'

His smile softened his features. 'Nor did I,' he murmured, brushing Ella's head with a gentle kiss, and the tender gesture turned her heart to mush.

Oh, Leo…

She showered and changed, then took herself outside, sitting on the bench in the cool shade of their east-facing terrace and leaving him to deal with Ella while she took advantage of a few moments to herself when she didn't have to pretend anything.

She'd tipped her head back and closed her eyes, but then she heard the gravel crunch, then the slight creak of the bench as he sat down beside her.

'Here. I've brought you a drink.'

She opened her eyes and sat up, taking the glass

of sparkling water with a slice of lime floating in it, the outside beaded with moisture.

'Just what I wanted. Thank you. Is she asleep?'

'Yes, she's gone out like a light. The swimming must have tired her out. Look, I wanted to talk to you about this weekend. Are you OK with me doing all this cooking?'

Amy looked at him in astonishment, puzzled that he would even ask. 'Why wouldn't I be? You're the one doing all the work and it's not as if I won't get to eat it. It's not down to me.'

'It is in a way,' he pointed out. 'If I'm cooking, you'll need to look after Ella, and it's not really why you're here. I should have checked with you instead of just assuming.'

'Of course I don't mind,' she said, puzzled that he would even ask her. 'You know I don't. Ella's lovely, and, anyway, I am here to look after her.'

'Only when I'm in meetings. That was the deal.'

'Leo, it's fine, and, as you said, you need to play around with their produce, try out some recipes, and I'm more than happy to help you in any way I can. I owe you so much—'

'You owe me nothing,' he said softly, his eyes curiously intent. 'I've told you that.'

She shook her head briefly to free her from the

magnetic hold of those mesmerising eyes. 'I do. Not just the catering. I'm OK with that now. That's just money, really, but—well, without you I would have married Nick, and it would have been a disaster. If you hadn't said what you did…'

His sigh sounded weary and dredged up from his boots. 'I had to, Amy. You just didn't seem happy enough for it to be right, and there was no way I could let you sleepwalk into a doomed marriage.'

'Like you did into yours?' she asked rashly, and then bit her lip and waited for his reply.

It was quiet on the shady terrace, the valley stretched out below them, the doors to his bedroom open so he could hear Ella if she woke. A light breeze whispered over Amy's skin, welcome after the heat of the day, and she pressed the cold glass to her face to cool it.

He glanced at her, then looked away. 'I didn't sleepwalk into it,' he said at last. 'Lisa did, to a certain extent, but I was railroaded into it by my own sense of decency. Lisa was pregnant, I was the father, I was responsible for her and the baby. I did, as they say, the decent thing. End of. Except that wasn't the end of it,' he added bleakly, 'and I don't know if it ever will be.'

He was staring out over the rolling hills, his eyes remote and shuttered, and she reached out and laid a hand on his shoulder.

'Oh, Leo, I'm so sorry,' she said softly. 'Want to talk about it?'

He glanced briefly back at her, then away again. 'Not really. Why would I? What's the point? It won't change anything.'

It was a less than subtle hint to drop the subject, but somehow she couldn't, so she pressed on. 'I know that, but you always used to talk to me, get things off your chest. I thought it might help you. You must be so sad, for Ella if not for yourself.'

'Sad?' He gave a bitter little laugh that made her wince. 'I don't think sad even scratches the surface. Gutted? Wracked with guilt? Ashamed?'

Ashamed...?

He turned his head to look at her, and in the depths of those beautiful amber eyes she could see an unfathomable despair. And then the shutters came down and he looked away, glancing pointedly at his watch.

'It's time we went over for dinner,' he said, changing the subject so emphatically now that there was no way she was about to argue with him. And that was that—the end of anything deep and meaningful, at least for now.

Just as well. She was getting altogether too interested in Leo and his thoughts and feelings, and it was time she remembered that it was none of her business, and that he was just a friend.

It's not wrong to take an interest in your friends. You were only asking because you care.

No, she wasn't. She was being nosy, delving into parts of his psyche that were absolutely none of her business, friend or not. If he wanted to tell her about his disastrous marriage, no doubt he'd do it in his own time, but it wasn't down to her to ask.

He got up and went inside, leaving her sitting alone on the terrace. She closed her eyes, tilted her head back against the worn old stone and sighed softly.

There had been a time, not all that long ago, when he'd told her everything. He'd poured his heart out to her on numerous occasions; break-ups with his girlfriends, rows with his parents—all manner of things. She'd done the same with him, and there'd never been anything they couldn't talk about.

And there'd been the good things, too, like the time he'd won the TV cookery competition when he was only nineteen, and his first job as a head chef when he'd scarcely finished his training, and his meteoric rise to success as a TV celebrity chef.

That was when his ageing father had handed over the reins of the company restaurant business, and he'd raised his game and gone from strength to strength.

But all the time he'd talked to her. She'd been part of all his ups and downs, but not any more, apparently. Not since Lisa, and the marriage that had left him, of all things, ashamed.

Why? Why *ashamed*? Of his choice of bride? His behaviour towards her? Because she'd died in such tragic circumstances? Hardly his fault—unless there was something about her death that she didn't know. And she wasn't likely to now, because apparently he wasn't prepared to share anything more intimate than a menu, and she couldn't believe how much it hurt.

CHAPTER SIX

AS THEY WERE seeing the others off the following morning, Massimo apologised for abandoning them.

'Don't worry about it, we'll be fine,' Leo said. 'Can I raid your vegetable garden, Lydia?'

'Oh, feel free, you don't have to ask,' she said wholeheartedly. 'Use anything you want, there or in the kitchen. Are you sure you don't mind doing lunch for us all? I don't want you to feel you have to.'

He laughed. 'Don't be silly, it'll be a pleasure and I love a family party. It'll be fun. And don't worry about us, we'll be fine, won't we, Amy?'

'Of course we will,' Amy said, but the butterflies were at it again at the thought of forty-eight hours alone with him. His accidental touch yesterday by the pool was still fresh in her mind, and they'd been surrounded then. What would have happened if they'd been alone?

Nothing, probably, and if there was another

awkward moment like that she'd only have to mention Lisa and he'd back off at the speed of light. She let out a quiet sigh and waved goodbye to the family.

'Right,' he said, watching the dust trail thrown up by their car as they drove away. 'I need to do some food shopping. There's a market on where we went the other day. Want to come?'

'Sure.' She flashed him a cheeky smile. 'I can defend you from all the old women who want to grope you.'

He chuckled and rolled his eyes. 'Oh, Amy, how would I cope without you?' he said softly.

'Well, aren't you lucky you don't have to?' she quipped straight back at him, and turned away so he didn't see the yearning in her eyes.

Ella fell asleep in the car, so he put her carefully in the buggy and plundered the produce stalls while Amy followed with Ella and captured the atmosphere on her ever-present camera. He found the butcher Lydia had recommended and got into an earnest conversation, which as usual brought out his lovely Italian side that was so irresistibly sexy.

He bought a shoulder of mutton, not something readily available in England, and three racks of lamb. 'I'm going to do lamb two ways for Sunday lunch,' he told her when he finally got away. 'Easy for the numbers, and tender enough for the kids to eat.'

'Yummy.'

'It will be. Even though you have no faith in me.'

She laughed. 'I never said that.'

His mouth twitched but he said nothing, just hung the bag on the back of the buggy and carried on, wandering along the stalls, chatting to people and picking up this and that as they went, and she strolled along behind him with Ella in the buggy, taking photos and pretended to herself that they were a couple.

'Right, I'm done here. Anything else you want to do before we go back?'

She shook her head, so they walked back to the car, him laden with bags, her pushing the buggy with that surreal sensation that somehow it was her place to do it. If only…

'It's getting hot,' he said, tilting his head back and looking up at the sun. 'It'll be a scorcher later.'

'It's hot enough now,' she said, happy to walk in the shade and wondering if everyone was looking at them and speculating, because everywhere they went he was recognised, and not just by women old enough to be his grandmother. She hadn't realised his fame was so widespread in Italy, but apparently it was.

And mostly he tolerated it with good grace, but she could tell that for once he would have liked to be able to walk around without people saying something to him, or nudging each other and staring. At him, or them together? Would it spark a whole lot of media speculation about his private life? She hoped not, for his sake, and she was glad to get back to the car and away from prying eyes.

He stashed everything in the boot, strapped Ella into her seat and drove home.

No. Not home. They didn't have a home, and there was no 'they', either. Just him and Ella, and her.

'I fancy a dip,' he announced, putting the last things away in the kitchen. 'Want to swim, baby?'

She opened her mouth to answer and then realised he was talking to Ella. Well, of course he was! Why wouldn't he be? He'd never called her baby. Never called her anything except Amy. And brat, on occasions, when she had been, which had been quite often all those years ago.

'Going to join us?'

Was she? She turned her head and met his eyes. They told her nothing. 'Do you want me to?'

He shrugged. 'Only if you want to. It's easier with Ella if there are two of us, but it's not strictly necessary if you'd rather not.'

Of course. He just wanted help with the baby, and put like that it was hard to refuse. Besides, she couldn't think of anything she'd rather do than dive into the cool, refreshing water, so they changed and went over to the pool, and he rigged up the tilting parasol so it hung across the water and they played in the shade with Ella until it was time for her lunch.

'Stay here a bit longer if you like. I'll get her dressed and feed her and then I might put her down for a bit,' he said, handing the baby to her for a moment while he vaulted out of the water, rubbed himself down roughly with a towel and then bent and took Ella from her and walked away.

She let out a long, slow, silent sigh of relief as he went up the steps and disappeared from sight onto the terrace. She'd put on the one-piece again that she'd bought on Wednesday, but she'd felt every bit as naked and as aware of him in that as she had in the bikini.

Because his hand had brushed her breast yesterday afternoon? It meant nothing, she told herself, just an accidental touch.

So why couldn't she forget it, and why couldn't he look at her straight in the eye any more? Or, at least, he hadn't in the past hour or so, since she'd been wearing it.

Stupid. So, so stupid. And it was changing the dynamics of their relationship.

She kicked away from the end of the pool, gliding under the surface with her arms stretched out in front of her until her fingertips hit the other end, and then she tumble-turned and swam back again, up and down, up and down, pushing herself harder and harder until her arms and legs were shaking with the effort.

Even Leo hadn't worked her that hard the summer he'd coached her to swim for the school relay team. And she was thinking about him *again!*

She swam two more lengths to get him out of her mind, then gave up and rolled onto her back and kicked lazily into the centre of the pool, floating with her face turned up to the sun and her arms and legs outstretched like a star.

It was gorgeous. The heat of the sun warmed her where the water had cooled her skin, and she felt all the tension of the last few days soaking out of her body and drifting away across the surface of the pool.

Bliss. Utter, utter bliss—

Something cold splashed onto her face, and she gave a startled shriek and jack-knifed up, frantically treading water while she looked up into Leo's laughing eyes.

'How long have you been there?' she asked indignantly, righting herself and glowering at him.

'Only a moment or two. You looked so peaceful it seemed a shame to disturb you, but I've brought you a nice cold drink.'

'Yes, I rather got the *cold* when you tipped it on me.'

'Drizzled. Not tipped.'

'Semantics,' she muttered. She stood up, cupping a handful of water and hurling it at him. It hit him right in the middle of his chest, and he folded in half and backed away, laughing as he tugged the wet material away from his midriff.

Oh, for the camera…

'I've only just put this shirt on!'

'You should have thought of that before you tipped my drink all over my face. At least I threw warm water at you.' She folded her arms on the side of the pool and grinned up at him cheekily. 'Well, come on, then, let me have it.'

He gave a soft huff of laughter and dangled the glass just out of reach. She stretched up, and just too late she caught the mischief in his eyes.

She should have seen it coming. She knew Leo well enough to know he wouldn't let her get away with soaking him. Even so, the icy flood down her arm and over her chest caught her by surprise, and she gave a strangled shriek and ducked back under the warm water for a second, coming up further away, out of reach.

She swiped the wet hair back off her face and tried to glare at him. 'That was so mean!'

Leo just smiled, set the glass down on the edge of the pool and retreated to a sun lounger a safe distance away. Wise. She swam over to the half empty glass and sipped cautiously.

Gorgeous. Ice-cold sparkling water with a dash of lime. Pity it was only half a glass now, but she wasn't going to pick a fight with him over it. She knew she'd never win. Leo always, always had the last word. She drained the glass and set it down.

'Where's Ella?'

'Napping. She was pooped after the swimming so I stuck her in the travel cot the second she'd finished eating and she went out like a light.' He tipped his head on one side and eyed her thoughtfully. 'Your shoulders have caught the sun again. Are you going to stay in there until you look like a fried prune?' he asked mildly.

It was tempting. The alternative was to get out of the pool in front of him, and she felt curiously, ridiculously naked, even in the one-piece, but she couldn't stay in there for ever, so she swam over to the steps where her towel was waiting, climbed out and wrapped herself in it before she turned round to face him.

'Happy now?'

'I was quite happy before,' he said deadpan. 'It was you I was worried about.'

'You don't need to worry about me, Leo. I'm a big girl now. I can take care of myself. And don't worry about Ella. I'll look after her, if you want to play in the kitchen. I could do with downloading today's photos and sorting through them.'

Anything to keep herself out of his way.

Picking up her empty glass and the baby monitor, she headed up the stone steps to the top of the terrace and left him sitting there alone, hopefully oblivious of the trembling in her legs and her pounding heart and this crazy, absurd awareness of him, which seemed to have sprung out of nowhere in the last few days…

Leo let her go.

Not that there was anything else he could do, short of grabbing her and hanging on, and that didn't seem like an immensely good idea right now. So he settled for watching the slight sway of her hips as she went up the steps, the beads of water on her shoulders sparkling in the sun.

His eyes tracked down to linger on those slender ankles below the smooth, gleaming curve of her calves. Her legs were browner. Even in the last few days she'd acquired a delicate tan from the glorious Tuscan weather. It was early June, hot yet still bearable, and Amy was flourishing, like a flower turning its face up to the sun.

And he was getting obsessed. He had ingredients to experiment with, the Sunday lunch menu to finalise, and he was wasting the precious time he had while Ella was asleep. He should be using that time wisely, not staring at Amy's legs as they disappeared up the steps and behind the parapet wall and imagining them wrapped around him.

And he should *so* not be thinking about her like that!

He groaned. He wasn't interested in Amy.

At all.

So why was he still watching her?

She vanished from sight and he closed his eyes and dragged his hand down over his face as if he could wipe away the image from his mind.

Not a chance. With a sigh dredged up from his boots, he picked up his glass, got to his feet and took her advice. Time to go and have a look at the vegetable garden, and then do something useful in the kitchen, instead of fantasising the day away. And from now on he was going to keep his distance and hope that also meant he could keep his sanity.

'So, my little guinea pig, are you ready for this?' Leo asked.

He was lolling against the kitchen cupboards, lean hips propped on the edge of the worktop, arms folded, a slight smile playing around the sides of his mouth, and he looked good enough to eat. He also looked more like the old Leo, to her relief, so she played along, trying hard not to be distracted by how downright gorgeous he looked.

Not your business! Nothing about him is your business, especially not that. Only Ella, and her care, and taking photos for his blog. Nothing else. He couldn't have made it clearer if he'd tattooed 'Back Off' all over himself...

'Are you ready for my honesty?' she said drily.

His warm chuckle filled the kitchen and made her insides melt. 'Oh, ye of little faith,' he teased, eyes crinkling at the corners and making her heart turn over. 'I just fancied playing around with some ideas and I didn't know if you were up for it.'

She shook her head slowly. 'Leo!' she said reproachfully, trying not to think about playing around with him or what she might be up for. 'When have I ever said no to you?'

'Oh, now, let me think—when I tried to kiss you?'

A distant memory stirred, and she laughed. 'I was eight!'

'I think you were nine, actually, and I was nearly thirteen—and as I recall, you told me not to be gross.'

She bit her lips to stop the smile. 'I remember.

I also remember when I was fourteen and wanted you to try again, but you never did.'

His eyes changed, becoming curiously intent. 'You were a child, Amy, a minor, and I was an adult by then, so, no, I never did,' he said.

'I'm not a child now,' she said, her mouth on autopilot.

The soft caramel of his eyes darkened, the pupils flaring as he gave her a slow, slightly wry smile.

'I had noticed,' he murmured slowly, and pushed himself away from the worktop, heading towards the fridge. 'So—are you up for this, then? I promise not to poison you.'

She let her breath ease out on a sigh. 'You've tried before.'

'I have not!' he said indignantly, but it didn't work because she could hear the laughter underlying it and her lips twitched.

His laughter was so infectious she gave up the struggle and joined in, the sensual moment pushed into the background as their old banter resumed. 'Oh, all right, if you insist,' she relented.

'Ah, see? You still love me, really.'

Her heart crashed against her ribs. Love him? *Really?* She *loved* him*? Like that?*

'In your dreams,' she said drily, and wondered if he could see her heart pounding in her chest.

She couldn't—could she?

Still grinning, he wandered over to her and hugged her briefly, swamping her in that brief moment with a welter of scents and sensations that sent her emotions into a tailspin, before letting go all too soon to open the fridge and examine the contents.

'Do you fancy a glass of fizz while I cook?'

'Now you're trying to get me drunk and kill my taste buds,' she said, her heart still jiggling after the hug, the word *love* echoing in her head like the aftermath of a thunderclap.

He just rolled his eyes and plonked a bottle down on the table. 'Some people are never satisfied,' he said, then set two flutes down in front of her. A quick twist, a soft pop and he filled the glasses with pale, delicately foaming Prosecco, put the bottle back in the fridge and starting pulling out ingredients.

She sat back in her chair, twiddling the glass, watching condensation bead on the outside as the bubbles rose and popped on the surface.

Did she love him? As in, *in love* with him?

Well, at last! You've taken your time to work that one out.

She ignored her inner voice, took a slurp of the Prosecco and tried not to sneeze when the bubbles went up her nose, then swivelled round to look at him, camera in hand.

'So, what exactly are you planning to experiment with?'

He shrugged, his broad shoulders rising and falling and grabbing her attention. How had she never noticed them before this week? Had she been utterly blind? Evidently. But not any more. She clicked the shutter for posterity. Or her private collection, which was growing at an embarrassing rate.

'I'm not really sure. I haven't come up with anything concrete yet.'

'Concrete? How about your rock buns?' she added to get a rise out of him.

He rolled his eyes. 'They were fine.'

'They were rocks, and you know it.'

He sighed softly, but his eyes were brimming with laughter. 'So they were a little over-baked. I was—what? Nine? And you've never let me forget it.'

'You must have been more than that.'

'Not much. Ten at the most. And you had trouble biting into them because you didn't have any front teeth, I remember that.'

'Yes, and you teased me constantly about it.'

'And you rose to the bait without fail. You always did. Still do.' He stopped teasing her and shook his head slowly, a soft smile playing around his mouth. 'That was a long time ago.'

'It was. It feels like another lifetime.'

'Maybe it was.' The smile faded, a fleeting sadness in his eyes, and he turned his attention back to the fridge, effectively changing the subject.

'So, what are you going to kill me with tonight, then?' she asked lightly, swirling her Prosecco in the flute and following his lead.

He shrugged away from the worktop and shoved his hands into the back pockets of his jeans, drawing her attention in a way that did nothing for her peace of mind. She captured the image. Not that she needed to. It was burned onto her brain, alongside all the others.

'I don't know. I just want to play around and get a feel for their oil and cheese, amongst other things. I've had a look at Lydia's vegetable garden, which has given me some ideas. I think tonight's going to be pretty tame, though, so you're safe.'

She didn't feel safe. She felt—confused. As if her world had slipped on its axis, even though, in reality, nothing had changed.

Nothing? You ran away from your bridegroom at the altar! This is not nothing!

But it was nothing to do with Leo.

Or was it? Was that why she hadn't married Nick? Because of Leo?

The thought held her transfixed, and she watched him blindly while her thoughts cartwheeled in the background.

He diced an onion at the speed of light, pulled cupboards open, inspected spices and herbs, chose some, rejected others. She could almost hear him thinking on his feet. A slab of bacon appeared out of the fridge, and he cut a thick slice and diced it rapidly into lardons and tossed them into a sizzling pan with the onion.

The aroma of frying bacon began to fill the kitchen, and her mouth was watering. Rice appeared, a glug of wine, some stock—

'Are we having risotto?' she asked hopefully.

'Looks like it,' he said with a grin.

Her stomach grumbled. 'Sorry. Smells good.'

'Twenty minutes,' he said, and while he stirred and added a glug of this and a drop of that, he pressed thin slices of ciabatta onto a griddle and stirred something else in another little pan that he piled onto the crispy bread.

'Here, try this,' he said, sliding a plate across to her. 'Tell me what you think. I've used their oil and olives.'

'Gorgeous,' she mumbled, and had to say it again because he didn't understand her first attempt.

'Didn't your mother ever tell you it's rude to speak with your mouth full?' he said, laughing at her, and she poked her tongue out at him.

'Is this all for me?' she asked, and he leant over and snatched the plate back.

'No, it's not!'

'Pity,' she said, watching as his almost perfect white teeth bit through a slice of the delicious *bruschetta* topped with some gorgeous sundried tomato and olive concoction topped with anchovies. She didn't know what she wanted more, the *bruschetta* or the man.

She stifled a laugh and picked up the camera again. If she had the *bruschetta*, she'd eat it this once and that would be the end of it. If she had the man, she could have the *bruschetta* any time she asked for it. And not just the *bruschetta*—

Heat shot through her, stealing her breath and leaving her gasping.

There was a squeak from Ella over the baby monitor, and she shot back her chair and got to her feet. 'I'll go, you're busy,' she said, and left the kitchen hastily, glad of an excuse to get away from him while she reassembled her jumbled thoughts.

Closing the door of their apartment softly behind her, she leant back against it with a quiet sigh.

Whatever the change in direction of her feelings, and probably his, it was perfectly obvious that Leo wasn't in the slightest bit interested in a relationship with her other than the one they already had, a friend helping him out by looking after his daughter. That was all she was here for, and she had to remember it and keep her overactive imagination under control before it got them both into a whole heap of trouble and embarrassment.

Or her, at least, because for all the banter Leo wouldn't even talk to her any longer about anything personal, far less take advantage of her shaky emotional state. Which, she was beginning to realise, was more to do with Leo than it was with Nick and the abandoned wedding.

She pushed away from the door and crept over to the bedroom, but all was quiet. Ella was lying on her front with her bottom stuck up in the air, and she was fast asleep.

And Leo would know this, because the monitor had gone silent. She closed her eyes briefly, sucked in a deep breath and made herself go back to the kitchen. Nothing had changed, nothing was any different, and it wouldn't be if she kept a lid on it. Yes, she loved him, but just in the way she always had. Nothing more, nothing less, and certainly not like *that*—

Liar!

'Gosh, that smells lovely,' she said brightly, walking back into the kitchen and ignoring the nagging voice that had far too much to say for itself. 'Really yummy.'

'Is she okay?'

'Yes, she's fine. Fast asleep.' She picked up her glass and peered at the dribble in the bottom. 'Any more Prosecco in the fridge?'

He glanced over his shoulder. 'There should be, unless you've already drunk it all. You can top me up while you're at it. I've been working hard.'

She arched a brow at him and chuckled. 'Don't

give me that. You could make that risotto in your sleep.'

His lips twitched, drawing her attention to their soft, ripe fullness, and she had an overwhelming urge to get up and walk over to him and kiss them.

No! What was she *thinking* about?

She did get up, and she did walk over to him, but only so she could top up their glasses. Then she retreated back to the table, sat herself down and concentrated on the power of mind over matter. Or head over heart, more likely. The last thing she needed was to allow herself to fantasise about being in love with Leo. Not that she was even thinking about love. Nothing so ethereal. Just at the moment, she was quite preoccupied enough with thinking about kissing him senseless.

She stifled a groan of frustration and impatience at herself, chewed her way thoughtfully through another slice of the delicious *bruschetta* and tried not to down the wine so fast that she fell off her chair. Getting drunk would *not* be an asset to the situation!

In the nick of time a wide, flat bowl appeared in front of her, heaped with risotto drizzled with green-gold oil and scattered with torn basil leaves, and Leo leant across her and shaved some slender curls of a wonderful hard pecorino cheese over it. She sniffed appreciatively, and got a touch of Leo in the fragrant mix.

'Wow, that smells amazing,' she said, bending down to hide the sudden flush of colour that swept her cheeks. 'Utterly gorgeous.'

Leo, sitting down opposite her in front of his own plate, couldn't agree more. She was. Utterly gorgeous, and he'd never really noticed it before the last few days. When it had happened, he couldn't work out, but it had, and he was finding it quite difficult to ignore—especially since the incident with her bikini top earlier in the week.

He frowned, picked up his fork and plunged it into the steaming pile of creamy rice and tried to blank the image of the pale swell of her breast out of his mind, but the delicate rose pink of her nipple, puckered with the cold, was seared on his retina, and he could still feel the soft jut of it on the back of his hand when he'd brushed against her yesterday, taking Ella from her.

Spending time with her was awakening something that had been dormant for months—years, maybe. Something hungry and a little wild and beyond his control that was flaring to life between them. Maybe he didn't need to ignore it. Maybe he needed to talk to her about it?

But not now, if ever. She was a friend, a good friend, helping him out when he was in a bad place and so was she. The last thing either of them needed was him muddying the waters at this point in their lives, but his body had gone stone deaf to the pleading from his mind.

'So what do you think of it?' he asked, watching her demolish the risotto. 'I like the pea and mint with the bacon, and I think their oil and cheese really lend something interesting.'

'Mmm. Not going to argue,' she said, scraping the bowl. 'Is there any more?'

CHAPTER SEVEN

WELL, HE'D MANAGED to keep the conversation on track, he thought with relief as the door closed behind her.

They'd finished their meal, and then he'd told her he needed more time to play with the flavours so she'd gone to do some more work with the photos, which didn't surprise him because every time he'd looked up for the past few days she'd had that wretched camera in her hands.

But at least she was taking his request seriously, he thought as he worked. She must have recorded every last breath he'd taken, but he wasn't going to complain because the results that he'd seen so far were far better than anything he'd ever managed.

He fiddled around in the kitchen for another hour or two before it dawned on him that he was just keeping out of the way until he was sure she was asleep. Then he cleared up the kitchen, which meant there was nothing else for him to do tonight apart from test every type of wine they produced.

Which would be a waste, he thought morosely, staring at the opened bottle on the table in front of him. It was far too good to use as anaesthetic, and the last thing he needed was a hangover in the morning. He folded his arms on the table, dropped his head down and growled with frustration.

He should have been tired—not tired as in just finished a nineteen-hour shift in one of his restaurants, but tired enough to sleep, at least. Instead, he felt restless. Edgy.

He glanced at the baby monitor. She'd left it behind when she'd gone, and he'd heard her go in to check Ella, heard the gentle murmur of her voice when Ella had cried out once, but now there was nothing. He could let himself back in there, pick up his shorts and a towel and have a swim without disturbing them. That was what he needed. A long, hard swim, to burn off that excess restless energy. And maybe then he'd be able to sleep.

Something had woken her. She wasn't sure what, but she realised she was hot and thirsty. Maybe it had just been that?

But her bedroom door was still wide open. She'd left it open so she'd hear Ella, as Leo had the baby monitor in the kitchen, but she would have expected him to close it, or at least pull it to.

She lay for a while and listened, but there was nothing, no creaks or snores, not a sound even from Ella. She slid her legs over the edge of the bed and picked up her phone, checking the time. Twelve thirty-four. He must be back, she just hadn't heard him.

She tiptoed out into the hall and peered into Ella's room, but his bed was undisturbed, and there were no lights on anywhere except the dim glow of Ella's nightlight and the slanting moonlight through the French windows. The baby was sleeping peacefully, bottom in the air as usual, one little arm flung out to the side, and otherwise the apartment was deserted.

Surely he wasn't still cooking?

Tugging on her robe, Amy walked barefoot across the moonlit courtyard to the kitchen and found it empty, the room in darkness. She switched the light on and looked around.

It was spotlessly clean, everything cleared away, the fridge humming quietly in the background. And the doors to the terrace were open.

She stood in the open doorway and listened.

There. A rhythmic splash, barely a whisper, but continuous.

He was swimming.

And suddenly there was nothing in the world she wanted more than a swim. She went back to her room and realised the more modest black costume was still wet, so she put the bikini on, grabbed her towel and the baby monitor, and crossed the terrace.

She could see him now in the moonlight, every stroke leaving a sparkling trail of ripples on the surface, and she picked her way carefully down the steps, dropped her towel on a sun lounger and slipped silently into the water.

It was cool, the air around sweetly scented with jasmine, and she let her breath out on a quiet sigh of pleasure. There was something magical about it, about swimming in the moonlight with Leo, the soft water lapping gently around her, the drift of jasmine in the air. Beautiful.

Romantic.

That was what Lydia had said to her. *'It's just gorgeous to sink under that water in the evening when the kids are in bed and the stars are glittering overhead. So romantic...you and Leo should try it.'*

Her heart hitched a little in her throat. It wasn't meant to be romantic. She'd just wanted to join him for a swim, but suddenly it didn't feel like that, with the moonlight and the silence. She was playing with fire, crossing a boundary into dangerous territory, and she had to go. Once he'd turned and was swimming away from her, she'd make her escape and he need never know she'd been there.

Except, of course, he didn't turn.

The best-laid plans and all that, she thought as he slowed his pace and coasted in right beside her, standing up as he reached the end, sluicing water off his face and hair and knuckling the water out of his eyes.

The water streamed off his shoulders, turning to ribbons of silver in the moonlight, and she wanted to reach out and touch them.

Touch him.

No! Why hadn't she stayed inside, left him alone, kept out of his way, instead of surrendering to this magnetic attraction that had sprung out of nowhere in the last few days and taken her completely by surprise?

She must have moved or taken a breath, done something, because he turned his head towards her, his eyes black in the moonlight, a frown creasing his brow.

'Amy?'

'Hi,' she said awkwardly, the word a little breathless and utterly inadequate somehow in these odd circumstances.

His head tilted slightly. 'What's the matter?'

'Nothing. Ella's fine, she's fast asleep. I came to find you,' she explained, hoping it sounded more plausible than it felt at that moment. 'It was late, and I woke up and wondered where you were, but then I realised you were swimming and I thought it seemed like a good idea. You know, as it's a hot night…'

She floundered to a halt, trying to bluff it out when all she wanted to do was run away. Or throw herself into his arms. Neither exactly brilliant options. Oh, why on earth had she been so stupid?

Leo let out a quiet sigh and sank back into the water, stretching his arms out to grasp the edges of the pool as he faced her from his position in the corner.

What sneaky twist of fate had made her wake and come down here to torment him? His fault, most likely, going in there to pick up his shorts and towel. Damn. Well, thank God he'd got the shorts on and hadn't decided to skinny-dip. At least this way he could hide his reaction.

'Sorry, I didn't mean to disturb you. I just didn't feel tired enough to sleep, and I was hot and sticky, and the thought of the water just tempted me.'

That, and the fact that he hadn't trusted himself to go back into their apartment until he was too tired to act on the physical ache that had lingered long after she'd left the kitchen. And he'd just about done it, and now here she was to undo it all over again.

'It's the middle of the night, Leo,' she said, her voice troubled. 'You must be exhausted.'

Apparently not. Not nearly exhausted enough if his body's reaction was anything to go by. 'And you're not? Why are you here, Amy?' he asked, a trifle desperately. It was a rhetorical question, since she'd already told him, but she answered it anyway and perhaps a bit more truthfully.

'I was concerned about you. You just seemed—I don't know. Not you. Sometimes it's fine and then all of a sudden there's this great gulf that opens up between us and it's as if I don't know you at all.'

She gave a soft, disbelieving laugh. 'And I don't know why. All the time I feel as if I'm walking on eggshells with you, as if anything I say can upset you, and you just won't talk to me. It's like you're avoiding me or something and I don't know why.'

Because I want you. Because it's inappropriate, messy, and I'm not going there—

'I'm not,' he lied. 'I do talk to you. I've been talking to you all day.'

'Not about anything that matters. And that's not like you. You've always told me what's wrong, and now you won't. So what is it? Is it me? And if so, why? What have I done to hurt or upset you, Leo? Just tell me.'

He sighed softly. 'You haven't done anything, Amy. It's nothing to do with you.'

'So why won't you talk to me? You always used to; you said it helped you sort through things, cleared your mind. I only want to help you…'

Her hand reached out and rested on his arm, her cool fingers burning him with a river of fire that scorched through his veins and threatened all his hard-won control. His eyes closed, shutting out the image of her fingers pale on his skin. 'You can't help me, Amy. You're just adding another complication.'

She whisked her hand away, her voice puzzled. 'I'm a *complication*?'

'That wasn't what I meant—'

'So what did you mean? What's going on, Leo? What's changed? Because it's not just me, is it?'

He let his breath out, a long, silent exhalation, and dragged a hand through his hair.

'No. No, Amy, it's not just you, and I don't know where it's come from or why, but I can't let it happen. I *won't* let it. You're emotionally fragile at the moment, and I'm a complete mess, but we're both adults, we've got needs, and what we're feeling is just a knee-jerk response. We feel safe with each other, we can trust each other, but it isn't safe, not for either of us.'

He gentled his voice, not sure how to handle this situation and desperate not to make it any worse. 'I'm sorry it's all gone wrong for you, and I know it should have been your honeymoon, but I'm not the guy you need to choose for your rebound affair, Amy, so don't humiliate either of us by asking me, please.'

Rebound affair? For a moment she was so shocked she could hardly reply. 'I don't want—'

'No? So why are you *really* here now, then?' He shook his head, his harsh sigh slicing through the air. 'I'm not doing this, Amy. There's no way I'm adding you to the list of things in my life that I'm ashamed of.'

Pain ripped through her, making her gasp. *He was* ashamed *of her?*

Like he'd been ashamed of Lisa?

He turned and vaulted lightly out of the pool, the water streaming off him in ribbons as he picked up his towel and the baby monitor and walked away towards the steps, leaving her standing there, her lips pressed tightly together, her eyes stinging with tears as she watched him walk away.

They scalded her cheeks, searing their way down, and she closed her eyes, turning away from him and holding her breath until the heavy silence told her he'd gone. Then she folded her arms on the side of the pool, rested her head on them and sobbed her heart out.

It was a good hour—no, scratch that, a lousy hour—before he heard her enter the apartment.

He'd towelled himself roughly dry and pulled on his boxers and a T-shirt, then gone out onto the terrace, sitting on the bench against the wall and staring out over the moonlit landscape while he drank the wine he'd picked up on the way over. Not a wise move, but he didn't care any more. He was over being wise. It didn't seem to be working, not for either of them.

The valley was flooded with a cold, eerie light, and he felt oddly chilled. Not that it was cold, it was just that the moon drained all colour from the surroundings and turned it into a mass of stark white, interspersed with menacing black shadows.

Under other circumstances, it would have been romantic. Not tonight, when he was sitting here waiting for Amy and wondering how long he could leave it before he went to find her. Because he would have to, he knew that.

Oh, Amy. What a mess.

What was she doing? What was she thinking? He shouldn't have left her like that, but he hadn't trusted himself to get closer to her, to reach out to her, because if he once let himself touch her, that one touch would never be enough and there was no way—*no way*—that he was going there. Not with Amy. He was a mess, his life in tatters, the last thing she needed when she was so emotionally fragile. Not even he with his appalling track record could betray her trust to that extent.

He heard a door creak slightly, the click of a latch, water running, the muffled sound of her bedclothes as she got into bed a few moments later. The doors of her room were open to the terrace, as were his, and he listened for any further sound.

Nothing. Then a soft, shaky sigh, followed by a dull thump—punching her pillow into shape?

He put his glass down, got up and crossed the gravel, standing silently in the open doorway. She was lying on her side, facing him. Her eyes were open, watching him, waiting for him to move or speak, to do something, but he couldn't. He had no idea what to say to her in these circumstances, so he just stood there and ached with regret. He couldn't bear to lose her friendship, and he was horribly afraid that was the way it was heading.

'What have I ever done to make you ashamed of me?'

Her voice was soft, barely a whisper, but it shocked him to the core.

'I'm not ashamed of you,' he said, appalled that that was what she'd been thinking. 'Amy, no! Don't ever think that! I'm not ashamed of you, not in the slightest, and I never have been.'

'But—you said…'

She trailed off, sitting up in the bed, arms wrapped around her knees defensively, and in the good old days he would have thought nothing of climbing on the bed and hugging her. Not now. Not with this demon of desire stalking them both. He rammed his hands through his hair and gave a ragged sigh.

'I didn't mean it like that. Really. Believe me. I'm sorry—I'm really so sorry—if you misunderstood, but it isn't, and it never has been, and it never will be you that I'm ashamed of. It's me, the things I've done, the people I've hurt.' He sighed wearily. 'I need to tell you about Lisa, don't I?'

'Yes, you do,' she said, her voice stronger now, making his guilt twinge, 'because I don't know who you are any more and I can't help you like this. Not really. Sometimes I think I understand you, but then you say something, and—it just confuses me, Leo. Tell me what it is that's happened that's destroying you,' she pleaded, her eyes dark holes, featureless in the faint light, unreadable. 'Help me to understand what's hurting you.'

He hesitated for a moment, then gave another quiet sigh. 'OK. But not here, like this. Come outside. Have some wine with me. I picked up a bottle from the kitchen on the way back and I need help drinking it or I'm going to have a killer hangover. I'll get you a glass.'

He checked Ella as he passed, fetched another

glass from the kitchen and went back out to the terrace and found her waiting for him.

She was curled into one corner of the bench, her arms wrapped round her legs. He recognised it, that defensive posture, shielding herself from hurt, the wide, wary eyes and wounded mouth making her look like a child again. A hurt and frightened child, but she wasn't a child. Not any more. And that just made it all the more complicated.

He sat down at the other end of the bench at a nice, safe distance, put the wine glass down between them next to his and filled them both.

'Here.'

She reached out and took it from him, her fingers brushing his, and he felt them tremble. 'So—Lisa,' she said, retreating back into the corner with her wine glass. 'What happened between you that's changed you so much, Leo?'

'It hasn't changed me.'

'It has. Of course it has. It's taken the life out of you. Most of the time you're fine, and then, bang, the shutters come down and you retreat. The only time you really relax is when you're with Ella, and even then there's something wrong. I thought at first it was grief, but it isn't, is it? It's regret, but why? What happened that you regret so much, that you're so ashamed of?'

How had he thought she looked like a child? She was looking at him now with the eyes of a sage, coaxing him to unburden himself, and once he started, he found he couldn't stop.

'I didn't love her,' he began. 'It was just a casual fling. She was part of the team on the last TV series. I'd never spoken to her, but she must have decided she'd like a piece of me as a trophy so she engineered an invitation to the party to celebrate finishing the filming, cosied up to me and—well, she got pregnant. I thought I'd taken care of that, but she told me much later she'd sabotaged it, and she didn't show a shred of remorse. And at the time she didn't seem shocked or upset by the surprise pregnancy. Far from it. Not until the whole situation became much more of a reality, and then she just went into meltdown.'

'So you didn't love her? You married her just because she was pregnant?'

He gave her a wintry smile. *'Just because?'*

Amy found herself smiling back, but she wanted to cry for him, for what she'd heard in his voice. 'You could have said no to her instead of doing the decent thing.'

'Except that it was my fault. She'd had too much to drink, I shouldn't have done it.'

'Was she very drunk?' she probed.

'I thought so, but she might have been acting. But then, to be fair, I wasn't exactly sober so it's hard to tell. It was quite a party, and I suspect my drink was being well and truly spiked by her. And that was only the first time. She stayed all weekend—'

'You took her back to yours?' To his flat over the restaurant? The place they'd sat and talked long into the night, over and over again? She knew it was ridiculous, knew he must have taken countless women there, but still she felt betrayed.

'The party was at the London restaurant. I lived above it. Where else would I take her?'

'Anywhere in the world?' she suggested, and he gave a rueful laugh.

'Yeah. Hindsight's a wonderful thing. But after the weekend I told her I wasn't interested in a relationship. I had the new restaurant opening coming up in Yoxburgh in a few months, so much to do to prepare for that, and I was trying to consolidate the business so I could afford to abandon it for a while to get the new restaurant up and running smoothly before the next TV series kicked off, and a relationship was the last thing I needed.'

'So—she left you alone?'

'Yes, she left me alone, sort of, for a few weeks, anyway. And then she turned up at the restaurant late one night and said she needed to speak to me, and she told me she was pregnant. I didn't believe her at first, but she had a scan six weeks later and the dates fitted, and she was adamant it was mine. And she was delighted. Of course.'

'What did your family say?'

He snorted softly. 'Have you never met my grandmother?' he asked unnecessarily, and Amy smiled wryly.

'Nonna told you to marry her?'

'She didn't need to. She listened to my side of the story, told me I'd been a fool to let it happen, but that I owed my child the right to have its father in its life. And she was right, of course. I already knew that. I also knew that the business didn't need the media circus that would follow if I walked away from a pregnant woman, and I knew she wouldn't keep it quiet. So we had a quiet wedding and moved up to Suffolk, into a rented house, so I could concentrate on the new restaurant.'

'Don't tell me. She didn't like it?'

'She didn't like it one bit. She'd thought we'd have a glamorous life in London, and she didn't take kindly to being imprisoned in a tinpot little backwater like Yoxburgh. Her words, not mine. And then Ella was born, and she was even more trapped, and she started drinking.'

'Drinking? As in—?'

'Heavy drinking. Getting utterly bat-faced. Night after night. I told her to stop, promised her a new house, said we could go back to London, split our time between the two, but that wasn't enough. To be honest, I think the reality of the whole thing—the pregnancy and birth, the move, the amount of time I was giving to the restaurant—it was all too much. It would have been too much for anyone, but she was so far out of her comfort zone that it was just impossible. And then…'

He broke off, the words choking him, and Amy shifted, moving the glasses out of the way and snuggling up against his side, one hand lying lightly over his heart. He wondered if she could feel it pounding as he relived that hideous night.

'Go on,' she said softly, and he let his arm curl

round her shoulders and draw her closer against him, her warmth reassuring.

'She came to the restaurant. She'd left Ella at home, six weeks old, and she'd driven down to the restaurant to tell me she was leaving me. It was a filthy night, sheeting down with rain, the waves crashing over the prom, and she'd been drinking. I took the car keys off her and told her to go home and wait for me, but she started swearing and screaming in front of the customers. I called her a taxi, told her to wait, but she walked out of the restaurant into the lashing rain and straight into the path of a car. The driver didn't stand a chance, and nor did she. She died later that night in hospital, and all I felt was relief.'

Amy's arms tightened round his waist, hugging him gently, and he turned his head and rested his cheek against her hair. 'I didn't love her, Amy, but I didn't want her to die. I just wanted the whole situation to go away, but not like that.'

'Is that why you're ashamed? Because you wanted her gone, and when she was you were secretly relieved? Do you think you're to blame in some crazy way?'

'I *am* to blame,' he told her emphatically, pulling away slightly. 'I should have made it clearer to her what our life was going to be like, but I knew she'd got pregnant deliberately, knew that she'd set a trap for me that weekend, so I suppose I felt she'd got what she deserved. But she didn't deserve to die, and I didn't deserve to have to go through all that, and Ella certainly had done nothing to deserve anything that either of us had done. Nor had my family, and the media had a field day with it. Don't tell me you didn't know that because I don't believe it.'

'Oh, Leo. I read things, of course I did, and I was worried about you. I tried to call you several times, but you weren't taking any calls, and your parents were really protective so I couldn't get through to you and I gave up. I shouldn't have done. I should have come and seen you.'

Her voice was soft, filled with anguish for him, and she turned her head and lifted her face to his, touching her lips gently to his cheek. 'I'm so sorry. It must have been dreadful for all of you.'

Her lips were inches away. Less. All he had to do was turn his head a fraction, and they'd be there, against his mouth. He fought it for seconds, then with a shuddering sigh he turned his head and moved away from danger. Not far. Just enough that he could still rest his head against hers but with his lips firmly out of the way of trouble.

'Leo?'

'Mmm?'

'I wasn't trying to seduce you earlier,' she said, her voice a fractured whisper. 'I really wasn't. I was just concerned about you.'

He sighed, his breath ruffling her hair, and his arm tightened around her. 'I know. But things are changing between us, and I don't want them to. I love you, Amy. I love you to bits, but I'm not going to have an affair with you, no matter how tempted either of us might be—'

She pushed away, tilting her head to stare up at him, her eyes wide with something that could have been indignation. Or desperation? 'When have I asked you to do that? *Ever?* When have I *ever* suggested that we—?'

'You haven't. Not in so many words. But it's there in your eyes, and it's in my head, and I'm not doing it, I'm not going to be drawn in by it, no matter how tempting it is to turn to each other for comfort. Because that's all it is, Amy. Comfort. And it would change everything. We've been friends for ever, and I don't want to change that. I need it, I treasure it, and I can't bear to think I could do something stupid one day to screw it up, because I will. I'll let you down—'

She moved abruptly, shifting so she was facing him, holding his face in her hands and staring intently into his eyes.

'No, you won't,' she said slowly and clearly. 'You've never let me down, Leo. I've let myself down, plenty of times, and I expect you've done the same, but you'll never let me down. You've just stopped me making the biggest mistake of my life—'

'Yes, I have, and I'm not going to let you—or either of us—make another one when your emotions are in chaos and you're clutching at the familiar because your life's suddenly going to be so different from what you'd planned.'

He took her hands in his, easing them away from his face and closing his fingers over them, pressing them to his lips before he let them go. He tucked a damp strand of hair behind her ear and gave her a rueful smile. 'You just need time, Amy. Time to let the dust settle and work out what you want from life. And it isn't me. It really isn't. I'm no good for you—not in that way. You don't really want me, you just want what I represent—the familiar, the safe, but I'm not safe, and

I can't replace what you've lost by not marrying Nick. I know what you want, what you've lost, but I'm not it.'

She nodded, shifting away a little, turning her head to stare out over the valley. After a moment she gave a shaky sigh.

'I know that—and I know I'm not ready for another relationship, especially not with you. I mean, how would that work?' she said, her voice lightly teasing now, but he could still hear the hurt and confusion underlying it. 'I wouldn't have my sounding board any more, would I? How would I know it wasn't another awful mistake? I made the last mistake because I didn't talk to you. I don't want to do that again.'

She turned back to him, throwing him a sweet, wry smile. 'Thank you for telling me about Lisa. And don't blame yourself. It wasn't your fault.'

'It was. I should have driven her home instead of calling a taxi—handed the restaurant over to the team and left, taken care of her, but I didn't, I didn't realise she was that fragile, that unstable, and because of that she died.'

'No, Leo. She died because she got drunk and did something reckless, with far-reaching consequences. Everything else stemmed from that.

You were her husband, not her keeper. She was an adult woman, and she made bad decisions. And on the last occasion it killed her. End of.'

'Except it's not the end, is it? I've got a motherless child and a career I've neglected for the past nine months—more, really. And there's nothing I can do about it. What's done is done. All any of us have to do is take care of the future, and I have no idea how. All I can do is survive from day to day and hope it gets better.'

'It will.'

'Will it? I hope so, because I can't go on like this.'

He stood up, tugging her to her feet and wrapping her in his arms and holding her tight, his face pressed into her hair. 'Thanks for listening to me. And thanks for being you. I don't know what I'd do without you.'

'You aren't without me. You won't be without me.'

'Promise?'

'I promise. Just keep talking to me.'

He nodded, then eased away. 'I will. Now go to bed. You need some sleep and so do I. I'll be up at the crack of dawn with Ella.'

'Well, good luck with that,' she said ruefully. 'Look at the sky.'

They stared out across the network of fields and hills, still leached of colour by the moon, but on the horizon there was the faintest streak of light appearing in the sky.

'It's a new day, Leo. It *will* get better.'

He looked down at her, her eyes shining with sincerity, the one person he could truly trust with all his hopes and fears. He bent his head, touched his lips to her cheek and then, as he breathed in and drew the scent of her into his body, he felt his resolve disintegrate.

He let his breath out on a shuddering sigh and turned his head, as she turned hers, and their lips touched.

They clung, held, and with a ragged sigh of defeat he pulled her closer, feeling her taut limbs, the softness of her breasts, the warmth of her mouth opening like a flower under his, and he was lost.

He couldn't get enough of her. One hand slid round and found her breast through the slippery silk of that tormenting gown, and he felt her nipple peak hard against his hand.

She moaned softly, arching against him, her

tongue duelling with his as he delved and tasted, savouring her, learning her, aching for her.

Her hands were on him, learning him, too, their movements desperate as she clung to his arms, his back, cradling his head as he was cradling hers, her fingers spearing through his hair and pulling him down to her.

He groaned, rocking his hips against hers, needing her for so much more than this, and she whimpered as his hands slid down and cupped her bottom, lifting her against him.

Amy...

Amy! No, no, no, no!

He had to stop. She had to stop. One of them had to stop. He uncurled his fingers and slid his hands up her back, but he didn't let go. He couldn't. He needed her. Wanted her. He had to...

His hands cradled her face, the kiss gentling as he fought with his warring emotions. And then she eased away and took a step back, out of reach, and he felt bereft.

Their eyes met and locked, and after an agonising second he dragged a hand down over his face and tried to step back, to put more space between them while he still could, but his feet were rooted to the spot, his chest heaving with the need that still screamed through him, and he tilted his head back and stared blindly at the pale streak of sky that promised a new tomorrow.

Could he trust it? Could he trust her?

She reached out, her hand finding his, their fingers tangling, and he lowered his head and met her eyes again, and saw nothing in them but honesty.

'Make love to me, Leo,' she murmured, and the last vestige of his crumbling self-control turned to dust.

CHAPTER EIGHT

AMY LAY ON her side, one leg draped over his, her head pillowed on his chest, her lips tilting into a smile of utter contentment and wonder as his hand stroked idly over her back.

So that's what the fireworks were like. The chemistry she'd dismissed. The 'amazing' that she'd never, ever found before.

His lips brushed her hair, his breath warm against her scalp, and she turned her head so she could reach his mouth.

He kissed her slowly, lazily, shifting so he was facing her, his hand sliding round her ribcage and settling on her breast, and she snuggled closer, feeling the jut of his erection against her body as her leg curled over his hip and drew him up against her.

He groaned, deep in his chest, the vibrations resonating through his breath and into her like the faint tremors of an earthquake. 'I want you,' he breathed raggedly. 'I need you—so much. Oh, Amy—'

He rolled her onto her back, their bodies coming together instinctively, surely, and she felt the first quivers of another shattering climax ripple through her body. 'Leo…'

'I'm here. I've got you…'

His head fell forward into the curve of her neck, his mouth open, his breath hot against her skin as he said her name over and over again while she fell, spiralling down and down, reaching out, clinging to him as his body caught up with hers and took them both over the edge.

Their muted cries tangled in the soft light of dawn, their bodies blurring into one, and as their hearts slowed and their breathing quietened, he rolled to the side, taking her with him into sleep.

Leo lay beside her, staring at the ceiling and trying to make sense of his tangled emotions.

All these years, he'd been so careful to preserve their friendship, to keep it platonic, to treasure the bond they had without crossing the invisible line between them. It had been so vitally important to him, his respect for Amy's friendship so deeply ingrained that it hadn't ever occurred to him to muddy the waters by sleeping with her. Other women had fulfilled that need for him, women who didn't trust him or depend on him or need him, women who wanted from him only what he wanted from them. Women who weren't Amy, or anything like Amy, because Amy was sacrosanct, untouchable.

Well, he'd certainly touched her now, the line well and truly crossed, and there was no going back. What he didn't know was what lay ahead, because he had nothing to offer her except the few scraps of himself that were left over from work and from caring for his daughter. And it hadn't been enough for Lisa, so why on earth did he imagine it could be enough for Amy?

He groaned silently.

He should never have kissed her, never have let her lead him into her bedroom, never peeled away the flimsy barriers of their clothing and with them the protective layers of their friendship, exposing the raw need and desperate hunger that lurked beneath.

He'd made a catastrophic mistake by doing that, but what an incredible, beautiful, exquisite mistake it had been.

Because he loved her, in every way, without reservation, and what they'd done had felt so right, so good, so pure and simple and innocent and—just *right*.

Oh, Amy. His lips moved silently on the words, his eyes drifting shut against the tears of joy and regret that welled in them. *Don't let me hurt you. Please, don't let me hurt you.*

But he knew he would. Somehow, some time, sooner or later it would happen. And it would break his heart, as well as hers.

Ella woke her, the baby's wail cutting through her dream and dragging her back to reality, and she stretched out to Leo but he was gone.

Oh.

She stretched and yawned and lay there for a moment waiting, sure he must have gone to her, but there was no sound from him and the baby was still crying, so she threw back the covers, found her nightdress and went to investigate.

'Hello, sweetheart. Where's your daddy?' she murmured, lifting the baby out of the cot and cuddling her close.

'I'm here. Sorry, I was in the other kitchen but there was something I couldn't just drop. Come here, poppet.'

He took her out of Amy's arms, his eyes brushing hers fleetingly, warm and gentle but troubled, and she gave an inward sigh.

'I know what you're thinking,' she said, sitting down on the bed while he put Ella down on the changing mat at her feet and knelt down. 'But don't.'

He shot her a sideways glance. 'How do you know what I'm thinking?'

'Because I know you inside out, Leo. You might have changed a little, grown older and wiser—'

His snort cut her off, but she just smiled and carried on, 'But you're still the same over-protective person you always were, and you're beating yourself up at the moment, taking all the blame, wishing you hadn't done it—'

'No.' He sat back on his heels and looked up at her, his eyes burning. 'No, Amy, you're wrong. I'm not wishing I hadn't done it. I just wish I could give you more, wish I could offer you a future—'

'Shh.' She leant forward and pressed a finger to his lips, silencing him. He kissed her finger, drew it into his mouth, suckled it briefly before he pulled away, and she nearly whimpered.

'You were saying?'

'I can't remember.'

His eyes were laughing. '*Shh* was the last thing.'

'So it was.' She smiled, and carried on. 'Forget about the future, Leo. It's far too soon to think about that. Forget everything except the here and now. We've got a few more days. Let's just enjoy them, get to know each other better, the people we are now, and have some fun with Ella. Have a holiday—'

'I have to cook.'

'You have to cook one meal.'

'And try out their stuff.'

'You're making excuses. I thought it was supposed to be a simple lunch?'

He smiled crookedly. 'I don't do simple, apparently. I want to do something that tastes amazing.'

'All your food tastes amazing.'

He arched an eyebrow. 'What happened to my critic?'

'Oh, she's still here, she'll come out when necessary,' she said with a laugh, and then sighed and threw up her hands. 'OK. I concede. Cook, play in the kitchen, and Ella and I'll play with you when we can, and you'll play with us when you can, and I know when they get back you'll be in meetings, but we'll still have the nights.'

She heard the suck of his indrawn breath, saw the flaring of his pupils as he straightened to look at her again, the jump of a muscle in his jaw. 'And then?'

She shrugged. She didn't know. And maybe it was better that way. 'What happens in Tuscany stays in Tuscany?' she said softly, and their eyes held.

'OK. I'll buy that for now.'

'Good. Oh, and by the way, you were amazing last night,' she said casually, and stood up to walk past him.

'So were you. Incredible.' His arm snaked out, his hand sliding up under the short hem of her nightdress and curving round her naked bottom, drawing her in against him. He rested his head briefly against her, his breath hot on her body through the fine silk, and then he let her go, his hand sliding down her leg and leaving fire in its wake. She sat down again abruptly.

'So, what are you doing today?' she asked when she could speak, but her voice was breathy and he tilted his head back and speared her with his eyes.

'I don't know. I know what I'm doing tonight. That's as far as my thoughts have gone for now.'

A lazy, sexy smile lit up his face, and she felt heat shiver through her.

'OK,' she said slowly. 'So—assuming we're going to do something a little more practical in the meantime, shall I shower first, or do you want to?'

'I've showered. You were sleeping the sleep of the dead,' he told her, that lazy smile still lingering on his delectable and clever, clever mouth. 'If you could shower now and take Ella from me so I can get on, that would be great. I'll make us all breakfast if you like.'

'I like. I definitely like. I'm starving.'

He rolled his eyes and got to his feet, Ella cradled in one arm, and he turned Amy and pushed her gently towards the bathroom door. 'Shoo. I've got a lot to do.'

'So, little Ella, what are we going to do while Daddy's busy this morning?' she asked. 'A walk? That sounds like a great idea. Where shall we go? The olive groves? OK.'

Ella grinned at her, a toothy little grin with a gurgle of laughter that made her heart swell in her chest until she thought it'd burst.

'Was that funny?' she asked, and Ella laughed

again, so that by the time she was strapped in her buggy they both had the giggles.

'What's the joke?'

He'd stuck his head out of the kitchen door, and she turned her head and grinned at him. 'No joke. She just started laughing, and it's really infectious.'

'Tell me about it. Are you off for a walk now?'

'Mmm. Ella thought we might like to go down to the olive groves.'

'Did she now?' he asked, coming over to them and crouching in front of Ella.

'She did.'

He chuckled softly, bent and kissed the baby and then, as he straightened and drew level with her, he kissed Amy. It caught her by surprise, the sure, gentle touch of his lips, the promise of heat in his eyes, the lingering warmth of his hand against her cheek.

'Have fun. I'll see you later,' he murmured, and waggling his fingers at Ella he headed back to the kitchen to carry on.

They had a lovely walk, the air full of the buzzing of bees and the scent of the olive blossom as they strolled along beneath the trees, and predictably the rocking motion of the buggy sent Ella to sleep, so Amy's mind was free to wander.

And of course it wandered straight to Leo, and stayed there.

Not surprising, really, after last night. She'd never felt like she had then, but it wasn't because of anything in particular that he'd done, it was just because it had been him—his touch, his kiss, his body. It had just felt—right, as if everything in the universe had fallen neatly into place when she had been in his arms.

And today the sun was brighter, the grass greener, the birdsong louder. A smile on her face, she turned the buggy round and headed back up the hill to Leo. It was time she went back, anyway. She'd been out in the sun too long and her shoulders were burning.

She left the buggy with Leo and went to put after-sun lotion on, and when she got back Ella was awake, so they played outside the kitchen until Leo called them in for lunch, then Amy took her back in the garden under the shade of the pergola until she yawned again.

'I'm going to put her down in her cot,' she told Leo. 'Do you need any help?'

He shot her a warm but distracted smile. 'No, not really.'

'I'll sort some more photos, then,' she said, and going up on tiptoe she kissed his cheek and left him to it.

She couldn't quite believe how many pictures she'd taken of Leo.

Leo cooking, Leo swimming, Leo laughing, frowning, smiling, winking at her cheekily—hundreds. Hundreds and hundreds. Lots of Ella, too, and the two of them together. They brought a lump to her throat.

There were others, of the family, of the *palazzo* and its grounds, the olive groves, the vineyards, the chestnut woods—anywhere he'd gone and she'd been with him, she'd taken photos. And she'd lent him the camera so he could take some when she wasn't there, and she scrolled through those with interest.

He'd certainly have plenty to choose from for his blog, she thought with relief, so she didn't need to feel she owed him anything, not by the time she'd added in the babysitting this week and for the eight weeks of the filming.

Eight weeks in which they'd do—what? She'd

said what happens in Tuscany stays in Tuscany, but if they were together, at home, would that still apply? Or would it be awkward?

Was their relationship going to end when they left Italy? She didn't know, and she didn't want to ask him, because she wasn't sure she'd want to hear the answer.

Then Ella cried, and she shut down her laptop and went to get her. She was sitting up in her little cot, rubbing her eyes and wailing sleepily, and she held her arms up to Amy.

'Hello, baby,' she murmured. 'It's all right, I'm here.'

She scooped her up gently and hugged her, and Ella's little arms snaked round her neck, chubby fingers splayed against her sunburnt shoulders. The tousled little head snuggled down into the crook of Amy's neck, and she squeezed the baby tight, deeply touched by the little one's affection. She'd formed a real bond with her in this short time, and it would be such a wrench not to see her again every day, not to be part of her life when this was done.

She was such a sweet child, and it was so sad that she would grow up without her mother. How would that feel? For all her gentle interference,

Amy's mother was a huge part of her life. How would it have been never to have known the security and warmth that came with being so deeply, unreservedly and unconditionally loved by the woman who'd given you life? Even the thought of it made Amy ache inside for her.

Could she take that woman's place? In a heartbeat.

Would she be invited to? As his wife?

'It'll be a cold day in hell before that happens.'

Oh, Leo…

She gave a quiet sigh and changed Ella's nappy, put her back in the little sun dress she'd been wearing in the morning, picked up her pretty, frilly sun hat and went to find him.

There was no sign of him in the kitchen, but there was a bit of paper propped up on the table with 'In veg garden' scrawled on it in Leo's bold hand.

She plonked the sun hat on the baby's head, went out through the open French doors onto the terrace and followed it around until she spotted him on the level below, in a sheltered spot amongst the orderly rows of vegetables.

She went down the steps and walked towards him. He was crouched down, balancing on the balls of his feet as he studied the lush mounds of greenery all around him, and he turned and squinted up at her in the sun. It would have made a brilliant photo, but for once she didn't have her camera.

'Hi, there. Everything okay?'

'Yes, fine. We just wondered what you were doing.'

Ella lunged towards him, right on cue, and said, 'Dadadad,' her little face beaming, and of course he couldn't resist that.

'*Ciao, mia bellisima,*' he said, his face lighting up with a smile for his little daughter. He straightened up, his hands full, and bent his head to kiss Ella, his eyes softening with a love that made Amy's heart turn over.

He was standing close enough that she could smell him, her nose tantalised by a slight, lingering trace of aftershave overlaid by the heady scent of warm male skin, and he turned his head and captured her mouth with a slow, lingering kiss. Then he lifted his head, and she took a step back and pointed in the direction of his hands.

'What are those?'

He glanced down. 'Zucchini flowers—courgettes. They're so pretty, and they're delicious stuffed. I thought I might do them as a vegetable. Heaven knows, Lydia's going to have enough of them,' he said, waving a hand at the rows of rampant plants he'd been inspecting.

'I'm sure she'll think it's worth the sacrifice. So what are you going to stuff them with?' she asked, trying to focus on something other than the scent of his skin in the warm sunshine, and the lingering taste of him on her lips.

'I don't know. I've got a few ideas. I'll try them out on you this evening.'

He picked up a basket overflowing with the things he'd raided from the garden, plucked the baby off her hip, settled her on his and headed back to the kitchen, nuzzling Ella and blowing raspberries on her neck and making her giggle.

He was so good with her. Good enough that the loss of her mother wouldn't matter? And what about when they got back to England and *she* wasn't around any more? Would that matter to Ella? Would she even notice?

Don't borrow trouble.

Amy followed them, the taut muscles of Leo's tanned calves in easy reach as he walked up the steps in front of her. His long shorts clung to his lean hips, giving her a tantalising view of muscles that bunched and stretched with every step, and she wanted to reach out her hand and touch them, feel their warmth and solidity, test the texture of rough hair over smooth tanned skin. Taste the salt on his skin—

Later…

He crossed over to the kitchen, dumping the basket of vegetables on the big table. 'Tea or coffee?' he asked, turning his head to look at Amy over his shoulder.

'Something cold?' she said, and he pulled open the fridge and took out the spring water. 'So what's the plan for the rest of the afternoon?'

He shrugged, those broad, lean shoulders shifting under the soft pale blue cotton of his shirt, the cuffs turned back to reveal strong, tanned forearms. He'd always tanned really easily, she remembered, part of his Latin heritage.

'I don't know,' he said, jiggling Ella on his hip. 'It rather depends on madam here and what she'd like to do.'

'I'm happy to look after her, if you want,' Amy volunteered, but he shook his head.

'No, it's okay, I haven't seen her all day and I'm going to need you tomorrow morning so I'm keeping you sweet for that,' he said with a grin. He unscrewed the bottle and poured two glasses of fizzy water, added a slice of lime to each and handed her one. 'Has she had her bottle?' he asked, and Amy shook her head.

'No, but it's in the fridge there. I thought I'd come and find you first, see what you're doing.'

'This and that.' He took the bottle out, hooked out a chair with his foot and sat down with the baby. 'So how have you been getting on?' he asked as he gave Ella her bottle. 'Did you look at the photos?'

'Yes. There are some really good ones that'll be great for your blog. They're on my laptop. There's a ton of dross as well, of course, but you can have a look later.'

'I'd love to, but probably not until after tomorrow. I've got enough on at the moment.' He gave her a wry grin. 'I hate to ask, but would you be able to keep an eye on Ella for a while later on so I can do some more prep? You can stay in here so she can see me, but I could just do with an hour or two to make up a marinade and get some risotto under way. I'll put her to bed.'

'It's why I'm here, Leo.'

His mouth softened into a smile. 'So you keep saying. I tell you what, how about a swim first?'

* * *

She wore the bikini, and when Ella grabbed the top again, he just smiled and gently disentangled the baby's fingers, which of course involved his own getting nicely into the mix.

He eased Ella away, met Amy's eyes and winked at her, and she blushed, which made him laugh softly.

'Later,' he promised, and her mouth opened a fraction and then curved into a smile that could have threatened his sanity if he hadn't already lost it.

And before he knew what she was doing, she slipped beneath the surface and swam towards him, nudging his legs apart with her hands before twisting through them like a mermaid. She'd done it before, hundreds of times when they were growing up, but not now, when he was so aware of the brush of her body against his.

'Boo!' she said, surfacing right behind him, and Ella squealed with laughter, so she did it again, and again, and again, and every time her body slid past his, grazing intimately against him until he called a halt.

'Right, enough. I need to get on.'

'We'll come out, too.'

She went first, reaching down to take Ella from his arms and treating him to the soft, lush swell of her breasts threatening to escape from the bikini that was proving so rewarding.

Never mind mermaid. She was a siren, luring him onto the rocks, and tonight was so far away…

‘Are you sure you don’t mind?’

‘Positive,’ she said patiently. ‘Leave her with me and go and make a start, and I’ll change her nappy and then we’ll follow you. I can take photos of you cooking, and give you the benefit of my considerable expertise as a guinea pig while I play with her. And at least that way I’ll get something to eat, because I know what you’re like when you start something like this. You get totally focussed and forget everything else, and supper will just go out of the window.’

He smiled, as he was meant to, and went.

‘So what’s that you’re doing now?’ she asked, carrying Ella into the kitchen a few minutes later and peering over Leo’s shoulder.

‘Broad bean, mint and pecorino risotto—it’s the stuffing for the zucchini flowers, a variation on what we had last night.’ He stuck his finger into the pan, scooped out a dollop and held it out to her lips. 'Here. Try it.'

He'd done it so many times before, and yet this time seemed so different. She opened her mouth, drew his finger into it and curled her tongue around the tip, sucking the delicious, creamy risotto from it without ever losing eye contact.

'Mmm. Yummy. You've put more mint in it. So are they going to be cold or hot?' she asked.

Leo hauled in a slow, quiet breath and tried to concentrate on anything other than the sweet warmth of Amy's mouth, the curl of her tongue against his finger, the gentle suction as she'd drawn the risotto into her mouth all too quickly. He turned away to check the seasoning of the risotto and gave his body a moment to calm down.

'Warm. Things taste better that way, often, and they need to be deep fried in tempura batter and served pretty much immediately, which rather dictates it.'

'They'd go well with the lamb,' she suggested, and he nodded.

'They would. And I could cook them at the last moment when everything else was ready to go. Here, try this. I've been playing with the topping for the bruschetta.'

He handed her a dollop—on a spoon, this time, since he really couldn't afford to get that distracted, but it was nearly as bad. 'OK?'

'Lovely. Really tasty. So what do you want me to photograph?'

He shrugged, his shoulders shifting under the shirt, drawing her attention yet again to his body. 'Anything you like. You tell me, you're the photographer.'

'I don't know. What are you doing now?' she asked, casting around for something to take her mind off his body, because even framing the shots for the camera wasn't helping. If anything, it was making it worse because it meant focussing on him and she was having trouble focussing on anything else.

'Marinade for the mutton.' He'd set the vegetables on one side and was pounding something with a pestle and mortar, grinding garlic and herbs together with a slosh of olive oil and a crunch of salt and pepper, his muscles flexing as he worked. 'I'll smoosh it all over the meat, leave it till later and put it in the oven overnight so I can shred it and shape it first thing in the morning.'

He stopped pounding, to her relief, pulled out the shoulder of mutton from the fridge, stabbed it all over with a knife and smeared—no, *smooshed*, whatever kind of a word that was—the contents of the bowl all over the outside of the meat, dropped it back into the oven tray on top of the chopped vegetables, wrapped it in foil and stuck it back in the fridge.

'Right. Mint jelly.'

She watched him while Ella was playing contentedly with some stacking blocks, clicking away on the camera to record it all for his blog. Most of the shots were probably underexposed, but she didn't have any lights or reflectors so she was relying on the natural light spilling in through the open French doors to the terrace, and the under-cupboard lights that flooded the work area with a soft, golden light that worked wonders with his olive skin.

And as a perk, of course, she got to study him in excruciatingly minute detail.

The mint jelly setting in the fridge, he moved on, pulling together the ingredients for a dessert that made her drool just watching him.

'Tell me it's going to be your panna cotta?'

He threw her a grin over his shoulder. 'Was there a choice?'

Of course not. It was one of his signature dishes,

and she'd never eaten a better one anywhere. Technically difficult to produce reliably—or for her to produce reliably, at any rate; she doubted Leo had any problems with it—he was making it with the ease of long practice, talking as he worked, and he was a joy to watch. But then, he was always a joy to watch…

'I'm going to turn them out and serve them with a compote of freshly sliced home-grown strawberries in their cousin's balsamic vinegar. I'm hoping I can talk them into letting me have a few bottles a year. It's amazing. It's almost a syrup, and it's—oh, it's just lovely with fruit. Beautiful. Works perfectly with it. I'll make a few spares. If you're really good, I'll give you one later.'

'I'll be really, really good,' she vowed, and he turned, holding her eyes for a second or two.

'Is that a promise?' he murmured, and it turned her legs to mush.

He finished the panna cotta, poured it carefully into the moulds and slipped the tray into the fridge.

'This kitchen's a joy to work in,' he said, and turned back to her with a grin that wiped the promise of dessert right off the menu and made her think of something much, much sweeter, powerful enough to blow her composure right apart.

And his, if the look in his eyes was anything to go by. Which was not a good idea when he was busy.

'I'll take Ella out in the garden in the shade. She's bored, and she loves the little sandpit.'

And scooping up the baby, she headed for the French doors to give him space.

Leo watched her go, let his breath out on a long sigh and braced his arms on the worktop. Why was he suddenly so intensely aware of her, after so many years? What was it that had changed for them? She wasn't a child any more, not by a long shot, but she'd been a woman for some considerable time, and it had taken this long for the change to register on his Richter scale.

And how.

But it wasn't for long. They only had a few more days here in Tuscany, by which time he would have sealed the deal with the Valtieri brothers.

Because he was going to. He'd decided that on the first evening, but he'd needed to know more about them and what they produced. And now he did, they could sort out the small print and he could go home.

He just had no idea where that would leave him and Amy.

CHAPTER NINE

'So I was right, then,' she said, trying to keep it light. 'No supper.'

'Don't worry, you won't starve.'

'I didn't think I would for a moment, but I have no doubt I'll have to sing for it.'

He gave a soft huff of laughter and carried on fiddling at the stove. 'Did she settle all right?'

'Yes, she's fine.'

'Good. Thanks. Here, try this.'

He put some things on a plate and set it on the table in front of her. Several slices of bruschetta—with the new topping, she guessed—and a couple of the stuffed zucchini flowers, dipped in the most delicate batter and briskly deep fried, then drained and drizzled in more of the heavenly olive oil.

'Try the *bruschetta*. I think this topping works better.'

She picked it up and sank her teeth into it, and sighed as the flavours exploded on her tongue.

'Gorgeous,' she mumbled, and looked up and caught his cocky grin.

'Did you expect anything less?' he said, with a lazy smile that dimpled his right cheek and an oh-so-Italian shrug that nearly unravelled her brain. 'Try the zucchini flowers. I tweaked the risotto filling again. Here—rinse your mouth first.'

She obediently drank some of the sparkling water he passed her, then bit the end off one of the little golden parcels and groaned. 'Mmm. Yummy. Mintier?'

He nodded. 'I thought it might work with the main course as you suggested, instead of potatoes.'

'I don't suppose you've cooked any of the meat yet, have you, so we can try them together?' she said hopefully, and he chuckled.

'Not a prayer. It's going to take hours.'

He picked up the second zucchini flower and bit into it, and a little ooze of the risotto filling caught on his lip and she leant over, hooked her hand around the back of his neck to hold him still and captured it with her tongue.

He swore softly in Italian and shook his head at her.

'How am I supposed to concentrate now?' he

grumbled, putting the rest of it in his mouth, but he was smiling as he took the plate and slid it into the dishwasher.

'I don't suppose the panna cotta's set yet?'

'You want some, I take it?'

'Absolutely. With the strawberries. And the balsamic. I want the whole deal. A girl has to eat. And you wanted my terrifying honesty, anyway.'

He sighed and rolled his eyes, muttering something about demanding women, and she smiled. It was just like old times, but not, because now there was something new to add to the mix, and it just made it even better.

She propped her elbows on the table and watched as he dipped the mould briefly in hot water, tipped the panna cotta out, spooned some sliced strawberries in dark syrup over the edge and decorated it with a mint leaf and a dust of vanilla icing sugar, and then shoved the plate in front of her, his spoon poised.

'I have to share it?' she joked, and then nearly whimpered as he scooped some up and held it to her lips.

It quivered gently, soft and luscious, the strawberries smelling of summer. She let it melt on her tongue—the sweet, the sour, the sharp, the…

fiery?—and let her breath out slowly. 'Oh, wow. That's different. What's it got in it?'

'Pink peppercorns. Just a touch, to give it depth and warmth, and mint again for freshness. So what do you think of their balsamic? Good, isn't it?'

'Lovely. Beautiful. The whole thing's gorgeous.' She took the spoon from him and scooped up another dollop and felt it slide down her throat, cool and creamy and delicious, with a touch of lingering warmth from the pink peppercorns and the fresh richness of the ripe strawberries soaked in the glorious balsamic vinegar waking up every one of her taste buds. She groaned softly, opened her eyes again and met Leo's eyes.

And something happened. Some subtle shift, a hitch of breath, a flare of his pupils, and she felt as if she'd been struck by lightning.

For long seconds they froze, trapped in the moment, as if the clocks had stopped and everything was suspended in time. And then he leant in and kissed her, his mouth cool and sweet from the panna cotta, a touch of heat that lingered until he eased away and broke the contact.

'OK, I'm happy with that. Happy with all of it, so that's it for the testing,' he said, backing away, his voice a little rough and matter-of-fact, and if it hadn't been for the heat in his eyes she would have thought she'd done something wrong

'Can I give you a hand to clear up?'

'No, you're fine. I'll do it. I've got more mess to make before I'm done.'

'Shall I wait up for you?'

He shook his head, and a slow smile burned in his eyes. 'No. You go to bed. I'll come and find you.'

She hadn't even made it to the bedroom before he followed her in. 'I thought you had more to do?' she said softly.

'It'll keep. I have more pressing concerns right now,' he murmured, and tugged her gently into his arms.

She heard him get up, long before the sun rose, when the sky was streaked with pink and the air was filled with birdsong. She propped herself up on one elbow and groped for her phone, checking the time.

Five thirty.

He must be mad. Or driven. This meal was important to him, a chance to showcase his skills to the Valtieri team, and of course he was driven.

There was a lot riding on it, and he wasn't going to derail it just because they'd fallen into an unscheduled affair. Even if it was amazing.

At least she didn't have to get up yet. She could sneak another hour, at a pinch, before Ella woke up. She flopped back onto the pillow and closed her eyes again, and the next thing she was aware of was the sound of knocking, then something being put down on her bedside table. She prised her eyes open and Leo's face swam into view.

'Tea,' he said economically, his voice gruff with lack of sleep. 'Ella's up and I need to get on. Can I drag you out of bed?'

She blinked to clear her eyes. 'Time?'

'Nearly seven.'

Rats. 'Give me five minutes,' she mumbled, and closed her eyes again. Mistake. She felt a wet trail across her forehead and opened them again to see Leo dipping his finger in her water glass again.

'Noooo,' she moaned, and forced herself to sit up. 'You're such a bully.'

His smile was strained, his eyes tired. 'Sorry,' he said, sounding utterly unrepentant. 'I really need you. Five minutes,' he repeated firmly, and went out, closing the door softly behind himself.

She looked longingly at the pillows, then sighed,

shoved them up against the headboard and shuffled up the bed. Five minutes, indeed. She groped for the mug, took a sip, then a swallow, and gradually the fog cleared from her brain. She had to get up. Now. Before temptation overwhelmed her and she slithered back down under the covers.

With Leo?

'Don't distract him,' she growled, and dumped the empty mug down and threw off the covers, just as Leo came back in.

His eyes flicked to her legs, then up again, and he zoomed in for a hot, quick kiss. 'Just checking you weren't asleep again.'

'I'm not,' she said unnecessarily, trying not to smile. 'Shut the door on your way out and go back to work.'

He backed out, pulling it to as he went. 'I'm taking Ella to the kitchen to give her breakfast while I carry on. That should give you time for a shower.'

The latch clicked, and she sighed and went over to the French doors and stared out at the valley.

Today was a big day for him, but it was also nearly the end of their stay. She knew Leo needed far more from her than a random fumble when he was too tired to think straight, but if she was going to be there for him for the next few weeks at least, to help him through the disastrous fallout from his doomed marriage, then her feelings and his had to remain on an even keel, which meant playing it light and not letting herself take it too seriously.

And certainly not distracting him when he needed to work, even if it killed her.

She showered rapidly and pulled her clothes on before heading for the kitchen. It was still only half past seven. How on earth was he functioning on so little sleep?

She found them in the kitchen, Ella mashing a soldier of toast all over the tray of the high chair, Leo doing something fast and dextrous with a knife and a rack of lamb. There was a pile of zucchini flowers in the middle of the table, and the air was rich with promise.

'Smells good in here,' she said.

'That's the mutton,' he said tersely. 'I got up at three and put it in the oven, and I've shredded it and rolled it up into sausages in cling film and it's chilling, and I'm just prepping the racks. She could do with a drink and a handful of blueberries. They're in the fridge.'

She opened the door and was greeted by shelves

crammed with goodies of all sorts, including the lovely, lovely panna cotta. ‘Which shelf?’

He turned and pointed, then went back to his prepping, and she gave Ella the blueberries and put a slice of bread in the toaster for herself.

‘Do you want a coffee?’

‘I’ve had three,’ he said. ‘Not that it’s helping. I’ll have another one.’

‘Or I could give you a glass of spring water with lemon in it and you could detox a bit for half an hour?’

‘Just give me a coffee,’ he growled, and gave an enormous yawn. ‘My body’s finally decided I’m tired. Talk about picking its moments.’

She laughed a little guiltily and handed him a coffee, weaker than he would have made it, longer, with a good slug of milk, and he gave her a look but took it anyway.

‘Thanks.’

‘You’re welcome.’

He took a gulp and carried on, and she sat down with Ella, leaving him to it while she ate her breakfast and tried to stop the blueberries escaping to the floor.

‘Tell me if there’s anything you need me to help with,’ she said, and he nodded.

'I'm fine. You're doing the most useful thing already.'

'I've brought my camera.'

'To catch me at my worst?'

She turned her head and studied him. His hair was tousled and spiky, his eyes were bleary and he had on yesterday's shirt and ancient jeans cut off at the knee, showing off those lean muscular calves that she'd recently realised were irresistible. His feet were bare, too, the toes splayed slightly as he leaned over, strong and straight and curiously sexy. Why had she never noticed them before?

She dragged her eyes off them.

'I think your fans will be able to cope,' she said drily, and pulled out her camera. One for her personal folder…

The family arrived back at eleven thirty, and Lydia came straight into the kitchen to ask if he needed help.

'No, I'm fine,' he said. 'All under control.' Unlike his emotions. 'What time do you want to eat?'

'Twelve thirty?'

He nodded. 'I thought we should eat in the garden under the pergola, unless you'd rather be in here?'

'The garden would be lovely. So, can I ask what's on the menu?'

He told her, and her eyes lit up. 'Fabulous,' she said. 'Bring it on—I'm starving! And I *will* be picking your brains later.'

He couldn't help but laugh. 'Feel free. Now leave me alone so I can concentrate.'

Not a chance. The kitchen became party central, but it didn't matter. He was used to working in chaos, and Lydia made sure they all stayed out of his way and she helped him unobtrusively, taking over the stuffing of the zucchini flowers while he checked on the other things.

Which was fine, except of course Amy was there, and his eyes kept straying to her, distracting his attention from the core business.

He forced himself to focus. The last thing he needed was the lamb rack overcooked or the zucchini flowers burnt in the hot oil when he started to cook them in a few minutes.

But it seemed that although she was pretty much ignoring him, Amy was very much aware of what he was doing, and with twenty minutes to go she chivvied them all outside into the garden to leave him in peace. He stopped her as she was following them.

'Amy?'

'Do you need me?'

What a choice of words, after all that had happened last night. He held out a serving plate piled high with bruschetta.

'Could you give them these—and try and make sure you don't eat them all yourself,' he added, grinning.

She took the plate from him with an unladylike snort and a toss of her head, and he chuckled. Still the same old Amy. 'Thank you,' he called after her, and she relented and threw him a smile over her shoulder as she went out of the door.

She checked her watch. Any minute now, she thought, and leaving Ella in Lydia's care she slipped back into the kitchen.

'Anything I can do?'

'Take the plates out and make sure they're all sitting down ready and then help me ferry stuff in a couple of minutes? I'm just frying the last of the zucchini flowers and everything else is done. The lamb's resting, the mutton's keeping warm and the veg are steaming.'

He was working as he talked and she glanced at the clock on the kitchen wall. Twelve twenty six. Bang on time. She felt her mouth tug in a wry smile. He'd never been on time for anything in his life until he'd started cooking professionally.

'OK. Nothing you want me to do except ferry?'

'No, I'll be fine. And, Amy?'

She turned and met his eyes.

'Thank you. For everything. I couldn't have done it without you. You've been amazing.'

She felt his warmth flood through her.

'You're welcome. And I know you'll be fine. They'll love it. You have some serious fans out here. Just don't burn the zucchini flowers.'

He *was* fine.

Everything was fine. More than fine, and he was in his element.

The food was amazing, and everyone from the babies upwards loved it. The zucchini flowers he'd finally chosen as the starter were beautiful and utterly delicious, and once the lamb two ways—*agnello in due modi* as Leo called it for the benefit of their Italian hosts—was on the table, he looked utterly relaxed. And by the time he brought out the panna cotta and strawberries, he was Leo at his best.

This was his dish, the thing he'd made his own,

and Lydia, who by now was muttering things about how on earth she was expected to feed the family after this, was begging him for a master class or at the very least a recipe.

'Any time. It's so easy.'

'Easy to make, but not easy to make taste like *that*,' Lydia pointed out, and he laughed

'But it's nothing without the right ingredients.' His eyes swung to Massimo.

He was leaning back in his chair, wine in hand, his eyes on Leo, and he nodded slowly. 'We need to talk. Heaven knows my wife's an excellent chef, and I'm used to amazing food on a daily basis, but you've taken our ingredients and lifted them into something incredible. We have to do a deal. I want our produce on the table in your restaurants.'

For a moment Leo said nothing, but then a slow smile started in his eyes and lit up his whole face. 'Thank you. I was going to say the same thing. I don't know what it is about your produce—maybe the care you take, the land, the generations of expertise, but I've been able to find a depth of flavour that I've never found before, and I really want to work with you. And I want that *balsamico* on the list,' he added with a wink.

They all laughed. 'I'm sure that can be arranged.

Nine o'clock tomorrow. We'll sort out the fine print,' Massimo said, and drained his glass.

She was sitting on the terrace nursing a cup of tea and watching the swallows when he appeared. Ella was in bed and the families had all gone their separate ways, and they were alone.

He dropped onto the other end of the bench and let out a satisfied sigh. 'Well, that went OK.'

She laughed softly. 'Did you ever doubt it would?'

'Absolutely. There are always doubts, but it looks as if I've achieved what I'd come for.'

'With bells on. They really like you, Leo. And if they hadn't, it wouldn't happen.'

'I know. Tell me about it. And I really like them, too. I trust them, and I couldn't have wanted more from this trip.' He turned his head, his eyes seeking hers. 'And I couldn't have done it without you.'

She looked away, suddenly awkward. 'I haven't done that much—'

'Yes, you have,' he said sincerely. 'I needed to know that Ella was all right, and she was, which left me free to see everything there was to see and take my time getting to know them. It's an important deal, and I wanted to be clear about what I was getting.'

'And are you?'

'Oh, yes. I imagine they'll want to tie up the loose ends tomorrow, but we're pretty much done. Time to go home. I've neglected my business long enough.'

Home.

Whatever that meant.

Amy stared out over the rolling hills and felt a stab of apprehension mingled with regret. She'd always known this was just for a short time, but it had been a wonderful time, cocooned in a dream world of sunshine and laughter and playing happy families. And now it was almost over. Eight weeks with Leo and Ella, and then she had to find something to do, some way of earning a living until her photography took off, and she had no idea where to start.

Whatever, it meant an end to her time with them in this magical place, and the thought left a hollow ache in the centre of her chest. Things had changed now for ever and, whatever the outcome of their affair, it would never go back to that easy, loving friendship it had been.

'So, what's next for you?' he asked, as if he

could read her mind, and she gave a little shrug and dredged up a smile.

'Oh, you know. This and that. I'm sure something'll crop up. I imagine there'll be wedding stuff that still needs dealing with, and I've got a lot of work to do on the photos for your blog, and pulling a portfolio together. I'll need to do some studio shots, clever things with lighting, that sort of thing. Arty stuff. Maybe I can do that while they're filming and the lights are there. And then I'll have to market it. Or myself.'

He nodded thoughtfully. 'I just wondered—I've been thinking I ought to do some cookery books ever since you first nagged me about it, but it's never seemed like the right time before.'

'And it does now?'

'Yes, I think it does. It will be a lot of work, but it might tie in well with Ella. And if I do, of course, I'll need a photographer.'

'You will. And you're right. I told you years ago you should do it but it just wasn't right for you at the time.'

'I don't suppose you want to take it on?'

'Being the photographer?'

Would she? It would mean seeing him again. Over and over again. Which would be fine if they were still together, but torture if they weren't. 'Mind if I think about it? I don't know where I'll be or what I'll be doing.'

'No, I understand that, but bear it in mind. I'd be really grateful. Your photos are amazing.' He gave a huff of laughter. 'There's just the small matter of a publisher, of course.'

'Now there I can definitely help you. I've got contacts, remember?'

'Great. Sound them out, by all means.'

He smiled at her, and her heart flipped over. Could it work? It would mean working with him again, spending time with him, helping him move on with his life. And moving on with hers. She knew a cookery book by him would fly off the shelves, and it would ensure her success, too, but more than that it would give them a better chance to find out if they could forge a future together.

'I'll see what I can do. I'd have a vested interest, of course, in getting this off the ground,' she reminded him. 'Always assuming I'm free.'

'I know. There's no rush. I've got the TV contract outstanding, and that'll have to come first.'

'They might want to tie them together—launch the book of the series, as it were. They do that a lot. Ask them.'

'I will. I'll sound them out, but they're getting impatient. The producer wants to see me like yesterday. I've told him I should be back by Tuesday and I can't deal with it until then.'

'Assuming tomorrow goes to plan.'

'That's right. So we need to fly out on Tuesday morning at the latest. Earlier if we can. I'd rather go tomorrow.'

'Another posh plane?' she asked drily, ignoring the sinking feeling in her gut, and he laughed.

'Probably. It's less stressful than killing time at an airport with Ella, and we need to pick the car up. It's easier. But we'll get whatever we can whenever we can.'

'See how it goes,' she said. 'I'll make sure all our stuff's packed ready first thing in the morning.'

'OK.' He reached out, threading his fingers through hers. 'I think we ought to turn in now. It's been a busy day and I need my business brain working for the morning.'

'Don't you trust them?'

He laughed, his eyes creasing up at the sides, that fascinating dimple flirting with her near the corner of his mouth. 'Of course I trust them, but they'll want the best deal and so do I. I need to be able to think clearly. I'm not going to sign my life away without realising it.'

He got up.

'Come to bed,' he said softly, and she nodded.

'Just give me a couple of minutes. You go first in the bathroom. I want to say goodbye to the valley.'

'Crazy girl,' he murmured, but his voice was full of affection, and he crunched softly over the gravel and went in through the French doors.

She let her breath out slowly. Less than forty-eight hours ago, they'd sat there together while he'd poured his heart out. And then he'd kissed her. Or had she kissed him? She wasn't sure, but she knew that from that moment on everything had changed.

Could she work with him on a cookery book? Maybe, maybe not.

She sat there a little longer, knowing they'd most likely be leaving in the early afternoon and this would be her last chance to soak up the time between day and night, that wonderful time when the swallows went to bed and the bats woke and took over the aerial display in a carefully orchestrated shift change.

She'd miss this. Miss all of it, but most especially the family, Lydia in particular. The warmth of their welcome had been amazing, and she knew it wasn't just because Leo was a celebrity. It was because they were lovely, decent people with a strong sense of family and loyalty, and she'd miss them all.

But most of all she'd miss being with Leo and Ella in this stolen moment in time. The little girl had crept into her heart when she'd least expected it, and Leo…

She sighed softly. Leo had always been massively important to her, but this holiday had changed things, shifted the delicate balance of their friendship from platonic to something she'd never anticipated.

She had no idea what the future would bring, but she knew it would be a long time before she'd be looking for any other man. Her emotions were a mess, her judgement was flawed, and it was far too soon for her to be thinking about another relationship, even with Leo.

Not that he was in any better shape than her emotionally, and probably a whole lot worse. The pair of them were a lost cause. Could they save each other and build a future together?

She desperately hoped so, but she had a feeling the answer would be no, once reality intruded.

She watched the swallows depart, watched the bats dart in to take their place, and when her eyes could hardly make them out in the darkness, she got to her feet and went inside to Leo.

Tomorrow would be here all too soon. It was time to go back to the future.

CHAPTER TEN

'SOON BE HOME.'

She glanced across at him and found a smile. 'Yes. Not long now.'

Not long enough. He'd booked another charter, not getting the benefit of the empty leg rate this time but there were bigger fish to fry, she guessed, like the meeting with the TV series producer tomorrow.

She wasn't complaining, though. This flight, like the last, had been seamless, the car ready and waiting when they arrived, and they were cruising steadily towards Suffolk as the light faded, Ella fast asleep in her car seat behind them.

She glanced over her shoulder at the little girl she'd somehow fallen in love with, and felt a sudden pang of loss at the thought of parting from her. From both of them.

Leo's face was expressionless, his hands relaxed on the wheel, his eyes on the road. He flicked a glance at her and smiled. 'You'll get a lie-in in the morning,' he said, with something like envy in his voice, but she'd swap her lie-in for a cuddle with Ella any day.

'Yes, I will,' she said evenly, trying not to dwell on how much she'd miss those special moments. She'd be going back home to her mother and he to his parents, at least until his house was finished, so at the very least their affair was on hold for now.

'So, when do you want to look at the photos?' she asked, clutching at straws. 'Shall I download them onto a memory stick for you? Obviously they'll need some work before you can put them in your blog, but you'll want to choose some initially for me to work with.'

'Yeah, that would be good. Maybe we could go over them one evening this week? I need to write it, too. I made some notes while we were over there, but to be honest I've had so much to think about my mind hasn't been on it at all. Not to mention certain other distractions,' he added, and she could hear the smile in his voice.

'Going through the photos will help,' she said. 'Will you be staying with your parents?'

'Initially, which'll make life easy when I go to

London tomorrow and have to leave Ella behind. I guess you'll be with your mother?'

She would, at least for a little while, and they'd be next door. Her heart gave a little leap of joy. 'Where else?' she said, trying to keep it light. 'In case it's slipped your mind, I no longer have a home.' Or a job, after the next eight weeks. Or Leo?

'It hasn't slipped my mind.'

His hand reached out and found hers, his fingers curling around it as it lay on her lap. 'It'll be all right, Amy. Everything'll work out, one way or the other.'

Would it? She desperately hoped so, but she didn't like the sound of 'other'. The uncertainty of her future was thrown into sharp focus by the raw reminder of her homelessness. And joblessness. Not to mention the touch of his hand.

'Does that apply to you, too, or is it only me you've sprinkled fairy dust on?'

He gave a short huff that could just have been laughter, and put his hand back on the steering-wheel. 'I'm a lost cause,' he said, which was just what she'd thought last night, oddly, but hearing him say it gave her a hideous sinking feeling.

'You're not,' she argued gently, her own situation forgotten because his was far, far worse. 'You've just been in a bad place, Leo, but that'll change. It's already changing. You need to start working again, doing more at the restaurant, getting back into the filming, focussing on your USP.'

'Which is what, exactly?'

She shifted in the seat so she could study him. He hadn't shaved today—or yesterday, probably, either—and the stubble darkening his jaw gave him a sexy, slightly rakish air. How on earth had she never noticed before this week just how gorgeous he was?

'You have great media presence,' she said truthfully, avoiding the obvious fact of his sex appeal in the interest of their mutual sanity. 'Everyone loved your first two television series. Another one will raise your profile, and you can cash in on that with the cookery book. You're a great communicator, so communicate with your public, charm the punters in your restaurant, flirt with the camera, sell yourself.'

His brow crunched up in a frown. 'But I'm not the product. My food's the product.'

How could he really be so dense? 'No. You're inseparable. You, and your enthusiasm for food, your quirky take on things, your energy—that's what people love.'

What she loved. What she'd loved about him since she'd been old enough to be able to spell 'hormone'. She just hadn't realised it until now.

'Well, how on earth would I market that?' he asked, and she laughed. He really didn't get it.

'You don't have to market it! You just have to be you, and the rest will follow. The TV, the cookery book idea, your blog—all of it showcases you. The food is secondary, in a way. You were doing all the right things already. Just keep doing them and you'll be fine.'

He grunted, checked over his shoulder and pulled out to overtake. 'Right now I'm more worried about where we're going to do the filming. The plan was to do it in my new house, in my own kitchen, but it's not ready and time's running out. I won't do London again, and they want more of a lifestyle thing, which will fit round Ella, but that's no good without the house.'

'So how long will it be before it's done?'

'I have no idea,' he said, and he sounded exasperated. 'The builder's running out of time, even though there's a penalty clause in the contract, but of course I've been away over a week so I haven't been on his case and I don't know how well they've got on.'

'What's left to do?'

'It's mostly done, it's just the finishing off. They were fitting the kitchen, which is the most important thing as far as filming's concerned, and it should be straightforward, but every time I think that it all goes wrong, so who knows?'

'Could you use the restaurant kitchen in Yoxburgh?'

'Not without disrupting the business, and it's going well now, it's getting a name for itself and it's busy. I don't want to turn people away; I have to live in the town, it's where I'll be working, so it's the flagship restaurant, and that makes it hugely important to the brand. It would be career suicide and I'm doing pretty well on that already.'

'So push him.'

'I will. I'll call him in the morning, on my way to London, see how far off finishing he is.'

He turned off the main road, and she realised they were nearly home—if family homes counted, and at the moment they both seemed to be homeless, so she guessed they did count. He drove slowly through the village, turned into her mother's drive and pulled up at the door.

He didn't cut the engine, presumably so he didn't wake Ella, but he got out and by the time she'd picked up her bag and found her key he was there, holding the car door open for her.

'I'll get your stuff. I won't stop, I need to settle Ella and I've got a million and one emails to check tonight. I've just been ignoring them.'

He opened the back of the car and pulled out her bag, carrying it to the door for her. She put her key in the lock and turned to thank him, but he got there before her, reaching out a hand and cupping her face, his thumb sweeping a caress across her cheek.

Her eyes locked with his, and held.

'I don't know what I would have done without you, Amy,' he said softly, his voice a little gruff. 'You've been amazing, and I'm so grateful.'

Her heart thumped, her face turning slightly as she looked away, her cheek nestling into his hand so his thumb was almost touching her mouth.

'Don't be,' she murmured. 'You saved my life, getting me out of here. I don't know quite what I would have done if you hadn't.'

'You would have been fine. Your mother would have seen to that.'

She felt her mouth tip in a smile, and she turned

her head again and met his eyes. 'Yes, she would, but it wouldn't have been the same. Thank you for rescuing me for the umpteenth time. I'll try not to let it happen again.'

And without checking in with her common sense meter, she went up on tiptoe and kissed him. The designer stubble grazed her skin lightly, setting her nerve endings on fire and making her ache for more, but before either of them could do anything stupid, she rocked back onto her heels and stepped away.

'Good luck tomorrow. Let me know how it goes.'

'I will. Enjoy your lie-in and think of me up at the crack of dawn with my little treasure.'

Think of him? She'd thought of very little else for the past week or more. 'You know you love it.' She turned the key in the door, pushed it open and picked up her bag. 'Goodnight, Leo.'

''Night, Amy. Sleep tight.'

It was what he said to Ella every night, his voice a soft, reassuring rumble. *'Goodnight, my little one. Sleep tight.'*

She swallowed the lump in her throat, walked into the house and closed the door behind her.

Time to start sorting out her life.

* * *

Her mother was pleased to see her.

She was in the sitting room watching the television, and she switched it off instantly. 'Darling! I didn't hear the car, I'm sorry. Is Leo with you?'

'No, he's got to get Ella to bed and he's got an early start in the morning.'

'Oh. OK. Good journey?'

'Yes, fine. It seems odd to be home.'

Odd, but good, she thought as her mother hugged her tight and then headed for the kitchen. 'Tea? Coffee? Wine?'

She laughed and followed her. 'Tea would be great. I've had a lot of wine this week. Wine, and food, and—'

Leo. Leo, in almost every waking moment, one way or another.

'So how was Tuscany? Tell me all about the *palazzo*. It sounds amazing.'

'Oh, it is. I've got a million photos I've got to go through. I'll show them to you when I've had time to sort them out a bit. So how's it been here?' she asked, changing the subject. 'I'm so sorry I ran away and left you to clear up the chaos, but I just couldn't face it.'

'No, of course you couldn't, and it's been fine.

Everyone was lovely about it. I went next door and spoke to them all, and the family came back here and it was lovely, really. We had quite a good time, considering, and Roberto made sure we had plenty to eat, so it was fine.'

'What about the presents?' she asked.

'No problem. I spoke to the store, and they agreed to refund everyone. They just want to hear from you personally before they press the buttons, and people will need to contact them individually, but it'll be fine. Nothing to worry about.'

That was a weight off her mind. There was still Leo's gift, of course, but she'd done what she could about that, and there was more to come. Looking after Ella for a week had been a joy, and photographing Leo had been a guilty pleasure, but she'd promised her help for eight weeks to help during the filming, and if that didn't come off, for any reason, she could give him those photos, edit them until they were perfect for what he needed, so even if she couldn't help him with a cookery book, he shouldn't come off too badly from their deal.

'Mum, are you OK with me staying here for a while?' she asked, before she got too carried away with the planning. 'Just until I get my life sorted out?'

Her mother tutted and hugged her. 'Darling, it's your home. Of course you can stay here. You're always welcome, and you always will be. And don't worry. Things will sort themselves out. I just want you to be happy.'

Happy? She felt her eyes fill, and turned away. 'I don't suppose there's anything to eat?'

'Of course there is! I knew you were coming home so I made curry. I'll put the rice on now.'

Ella wouldn't settle.

He couldn't blame her. She'd been trapped in her baby seat for a long time today, one way and another, and she'd slept for a lot of it. Not surprisingly, she wanted to play.

With him.

Again, he couldn't blame her. She hadn't seen nearly as much of him as usual in the past week, and she'd been in a strange place, with a strange carer. Not that she'd seemed to mind. She adored Amy.

His daughter had good taste. Excellent taste.

He covered his eyes and wondered how long it

would take to get her out of his system. A week? A month?

A lifetime?

'Boo!'

Ella giggled and crawled up to him, pulling his hands off his face again and prising his eyes open. He winced, lifted her out of range and opened them, to her great delight. Another giggle, another bounce up and down on his lap, another launch at his face. She was so easily pleased, the reward of her smile out of all proportion to the effort he was putting in.

He reeled her in and hugged her, pushing her T-shirt up and blowing a raspberry on her bare tummy and making her shriek with laughter.

His email was squatting in his inbox like a malevolent toad, and he had phone calls to make and things to do, but he didn't care. The most important thing was checking in with the restaurant, but they were shut on Monday nights so that wasn't a problem for today.

She pulled up her little T-shirt again and shoved her tummy in the air, and he surrendered. Ella wanted her father and, dammit, he wanted her, too. The rest would keep.

* * *

She stood at her bedroom window, staring across at Leo's family home. The light was on in his bedroom, and through the open window she could hear Ella's little shriek of laughter and Leo's answering growl.

They were playing. That wouldn't please him, with all he had to do, but they sounded as if they were having fun, or at least Ella was.

She couldn't help smiling, but it was a bittersweet smile. She already missed them so much. Watching him playing with Ella, focussing all that charismatic charm on his little girl, not caring at all that he was making an idiot of himself.

Oh, Leo.

It was warm, but she closed the window anyway. She didn't need to torture herself by listening to them. It was bad enough without that.

She turned and scanned the room.

Her wedding dress was gone, of course, hung up in another room, she imagined, together with the veil and shoes. And her ring? She'd left it on the dressing table, and that was where she found it. Her mother had put it back in the box, but left it out for her to deal with.

She'd send it back to Nick, of course. It was the

least she could do, it must have cost him a fortune. Not that he was exactly strapped for cash, but that wasn't the point.

She got out her laptop, plugged in the memory card from the camera and propped herself on the bed against a pile of pillows. She'd have a quick look through the photos before she went to bed, but she wasn't even going to attempt her emails. No doubt her inbox was full of sympathetic or slightly sarky comments about the wedding fiasco, and she might just delete the lot. Tomorrow.

Tonight, she was looking at photos.

'Are you busy?'

Busy? Why should she be busy? All she'd had to do today was draft a letter to all the guests, hand-write them and take them to the post office. Preferably not in the village so she didn't have to stand in the queue and answer questions or endure sympathetic glances. And sort through the photos.

So far, she hadn't even got past first base.

'No, I'm not busy. Why?'

'I just wondered. I'm back, I've put Ella to bed and I've got a site meeting with the builder in half an hour, but then I thought we could go through the photos.'

Ah. She hadn't got far last night. About five minutes in she'd been reduced to tears, and she'd had to shut her laptop. 'I haven't had time to go through them yet and delete the dross.' Or extract the ones that were for her eyes only. There were a lot of those. And it had been nothing to do with time.

'That's fine. We can do it together.'

'Here, or yours?'

'How about the new house? The builder said it was habitable, pretty much, so we could take the laptop over there.'

She could always say no—tell him she was tired or something. Except that so far today she'd done almost nothing. A bit of laundry, a lot of wallowing in self-pity and kicking herself for being stupid didn't count. And at least it would deal with the photos.

'Fine,' she agreed, dying to get a look at his house and too weak to say no.

'Great. Come round when you're ready, and we'll go from here.'

That meant seeing his parents, and they'd been the ones with the marquee in the garden, the catering team crawling all over the place, the mess left behind afterwards. And all for nothing.

She'd been going to take them something by way of apology, but now he'd short-circuited her plans and she wouldn't have a chance.

She shook her head in defeat.

'OK. I'll be round in a minute.'

'We're in the kitchen. Come through the fence.'

So she did. Through the gate in the fence that their fathers had made together years ago, and into their back garden where just over a week ago there had been a marquee for her wedding. You couldn't tell. The garden was immaculate, a riot of colour and scent. The perfect setting for a wedding.

She turned her back on it, walked in through the kitchen door and straight into Mrs Zacharelli's arms.

'Welcome home, Amy,' she said, and hugged her hard.

Amy's eyes welled, and she swallowed hard and tried not to cry. 'I'm so sorry—' she began, but then the tears got the better of her and Mrs Zach hugged her again before she was elbowed out of the way by her husband. He hauled Amy into a bear hug and cradled her head like a child.

'Enough of that,' he said. 'No tears. It was the right thing to do.'

'But you did so much for me,' she protested.

'It was nothing. Sit. Drink. We're celebrating.'

He let her go, pushed her into a chair and thrust a glass into her hand. Prosecco? 'Celebrating what?'

'Leo hasn't told you? They're starting filming the new television series next week.'

She turned her head and met his eyes. 'Really? So quick? What about your house?'

'We'll see. The builder says it'll be ready. Drink up, or we're going to be late.'

It was beautiful.

Stunning. She vaguely remembered seeing the cliff-top house in the past, but it had been nothing to get excited about. Now—well, now it was amazing.

While Leo poked and prodded and asked the builder questions about things she didn't know anything about, she drifted from room to room, her eyes drawn constantly to the sea, wondering how on earth she'd thought that Palazzo Valtieri could trump this. Oh, it was hugely impressive, steeped in history and lovingly cared for, but there was none of the light and space and freedom that she felt in this house, and she knew where she'd rather live.

He found her upstairs in one of the bedrooms. 'So, what do you think?'

'I think you need to give me a guided tour before I can possibly judge.'

His mouth kicked up in a smile, and he shook his head slowly. 'Going to make me wait? I might have known it. You always were a tease. So…' He waved his arm. 'This is my bedroom.'

'I see you chose the one with the lousy sea view.'

He chuckled and moved on. 'Bathroom through there, walk-in wardrobe, then this is the principal guest room—'

'Another dreadful view,' she said drily, and followed him through to Ella's bedroom.

'Oh! Who painted the mural? It's lovely!'

He rubbed his hand over the back of his neck and gave a soft laugh. 'I did. I wanted her room to be special, and I thought it was something I could do for her, something personal. I'm sure I could have paid a professional to do it much better, but somehow that didn't seem right.'

Her eyes filled, and she ran her fingertips lightly over the intertwining branches of a magical tree that scrambled up the wall and across the ceiling, sheltering the corner where she imagined the cot would go.

'It's wonderful,' she said, her voice choked. 'She's a lucky little girl.'

'I wouldn't go that far, but I do my best under the circumstances.'

He turned away, walking out of the room and down the stairs, and she followed him—through the hall, a sitting room with a sea view, a study fitted out with desk and shelves and storage facing the front garden and the drive this time, a cloakroom with coat storage and somewhere to park Ella's buggy—and then back across the hall into the main event, a huge room that opened out to the deck and the garden beyond.

Literally. The far wall was entirely glass, panels that would slide away to let the outside in, and right in the centre of the room was the kitchen.

And what a kitchen! Matte dark grey units, pale wood worktops, sleek integrated ovens, in the plural—and maybe a coffee maker, a steam oven, a microwave—she had no idea, but a bank of them, anyway, set into tall units at one side that no doubt would house all manner of pots and pans and ingredients as well. There was a huge American-style fridge freezer, still wrapped but standing by the slot designed to take it, and he told her it was to be plumbed in tomorrow.

'So—the verdict?'

She gave an indifferent shrug, and then relented, her smile refusing to hide. 'Stunning. It's absolutely stunning, Leo. Really, really lovely.'

'So who wins?'

She laughed softly and turned to face him. 'It grieves me to admit it, but you do. By a mile.'

His eyes creased into a smile, and he let out a quiet huff of laughter. 'Don't ever tell them that.'

'Oh, I wouldn't be so rude, and it's very beautiful, but this…'

'Yeah. I love it, too. I wasn't sure I would, because of the circumstances, but I do. I started planning it before Lisa died, but she had no interest in it, no input—nothing. And it's changed out of all recognition.'

'So she's not here.'

'No. And she's never been here. Not once. She wouldn't set foot in it. And now I'm glad, because it isn't—'

He broke off, but the word 'tainted' hovered in the air between them.

She took a breath, moved the conversation on,

away from the past. 'So, will it be ready for filming on Monday?'

He shrugged, that wonderful Latin shrug that unravelled her every time, and his mouth quirked into a smile. 'He tells me it's done, all bar the fridge-freezer plumbing and the carpets, which are booked for tomorrow. I've gone over everything with him this evening to make sure it's OK, and I can move in whenever I want.'

'Oh. Wow. That was quick,' she said, and was appalled at the sense of loss. She'd thought they'd be next door with his parents, but now they wouldn't. He and Ella would move into their wonderful new house a few miles up the road, and she'd hardly see them.

Oh, well. It had to happen sooner or later.

'It had to be. The series team liked the Tuscany idea, by the way, and it's a brilliant opportunity to showcase the Valtieri produce, so they won't be unhappy with that. I just need to knock up some recipes, bearing in mind the schedule's pretty tight.'

'So you're going to be really busy setting it all up this week. Do you want me to look after Ella from now on?'

He ran his hand round the back of his neck.

'Yeah, I need to talk to you about that. We'll be filming all day from Monday, and I need to spend some time in the restaurant in the evenings, and I can't do that and look after her. She loves you, she's happy with you—but I don't know how you'd feel about moving in.'

'Moving in? Here? With you?'

He shrugged. 'Not—with me. Not in that way. I just think it would be easier all round if you were here, but you don't have to do it. You don't have to do any of it. It was never part of the deal.'

'I changed the deal. And you agreed it.'

'And then we moved the goalposts into another galaxy. You have every right to refuse, if you want to.' His face softened into a wry smile. 'I'm hoping you won't because my parents need a holiday and I'd like to cut them some slack. They've been incredible for the past nine months, and I'm very conscious that I've taken advantage, but I know that moving in with me is a huge step for you, and I'm very conscious of what you said about what happened in Tuscany—'

'Stays in Tuscany?' she finished for him. 'That's not set in stone.'

'But we could still do that. Keep our distance, get to know each other better before we invest too much in this relationship, because we're not the people we were.'

'So what do you want to know about me?'

'Whether or not you can live with me would be a good start.'

'We seem to have done a pretty good job of it this week.'

'We haven't shared the toothpaste yet,' he said, his mouth wry.

'We've done everything else.'

'No, we haven't. We haven't been together while I've been running the business, which takes a hell of a lot of my time, and what's left belongs to Ella. And that's not negotiable.'

'I know that, Leo, and I can handle your schedule. I've already proved that. I'm not a needy child, and I'm not Lisa. I haven't been transplanted into an alien environment. I've got friends and family in the area, a life of my own. Don't worry, I'll find plenty to do.'

'I still think we need to try it. And to do that, I'd need you living here, at least while my parents are away, and preferably for the whole time we're filming. If you could.'

She hesitated, part of her aching to be there helping him and spending time with Ella, making sure she was safe and happy, the other part wary of exposing herself to hurt.

No contest.

'So how long is it? Is it eight weeks, as you thought?'

'I don't know. They're talking about eight episodes. Probably a couple of days for each, plus prep and downtime for me while they cut and fiddle about with it. I reckon a week an episode. That's what it was last time. Or maybe six, at a push. It's a serious commitment. And it's a lot to ask—too much for my mother and father, even if they weren't going on holiday.'

Eight weeks of working with him, keeping Ella out of the way yet close enough at hand that he could see her whenever he had a chance. Eight weeks of sleeping with him every night? Maybe. Which meant eight more weeks to get to know him better, and fall deeper and deeper in love with both of them.

And at the end—what then?

She hesitated for so long that he let out a long, slow sigh and raked his hands through his hair.

'Amy, if you really can't, then I'll find another way,' he said softly. 'I don't want to put you under pressure or take advantage of you and it doesn't change things between us at all. I still want to get to know you better, but if you aren't sure you want to do it, I'll get a nanny—a childminder. Something. A nursery.'

'Not at such short notice,' she told him. 'Even I know that. Anyone who's any good won't be able to do it, not with the restaurant hours as well.' She sighed, closed her eyes briefly and then opened them to find him watching her intently.

'So where does that leave us?' he asked.

'With me?'

'So—is that a yes?'

She tried to smile, but it slipped a little, the fear of making yet another catastrophic mistake so soon after the last one looming in her mind. 'Yes, it's a yes. Just remind me again—why it is that you *always* get your own way?' she murmured, and he laughed and pulled her into his arms and gave her a brief but heartfelt hug.

'Thank you. Now all I have to do is get the furniture delivered and we can move in and get on with our lives.'

Well, he could. Hers, yet again, was being put on hold, but she owed him so much for so many years of selfless support that another eight weeks of her life was nothing—especially since it would give them a chance to see if their relationship would survive the craziness that was his life.

She'd just have to hope she could survive it. Not the eight weeks, that would be fine. But the aftermath, the fallout when the series was filmed, the crew had left and he'd decided he couldn't live with her?

What on earth had she let herself in for?

CHAPTER ELEVEN

THEY WERE IN.

He looked around at his home—their home, his and Ella's and maybe Amy's—and let out a long, quiet sigh of relief. It had been a long time coming, but at last they were here.

Ella was safely tucked up in her cot in her new room, his parents had stayed long enough to toast the move, and now it was all his.

He poured himself a glass of wine, walked out onto the deck and sat down on the steps, staring out over the sea. He was shattered. Everything had been delivered, unpacked and put in place, and all he'd had to do was point.

In theory.

And tomorrow the contents of the store cupboards in the kitchen were being delivered and he could start working on some recipes.

But tonight he had to draft his Tuscan tour blog. Starting with the photos, because they hadn't got round to them on Tuesday night and he hadn't had a spare second since. Amy was coming round shortly with her laptop, and they were going through them together. Assuming he could keep his eyes open.

The doorbell rang, and he put his glass down and let her in. He wanted to pull her into his arms and kiss her, but with what had happened in Tuscany and all that, he really wanted to give their relationship a chance.

'Did she go down all right?'

He smiled wryly. Typical Amy, to worry about Ella first. 'Fine. She was pooped. I don't know what you did with her all day, but she was out of it.'

She laughed, and the sound rippled through him like clear spring water. 'We just played in the garden, and then we went for a walk by the beach, and she puggled about in the sand for a bit. We had a lovely day. How did you get on?'

'Oh, you know what moving's like. I'll spend the next six months trying to find things and groping for light switches in the dark. Come on through, I'm having a glass of wine on the deck.'

'Can we do it in the kitchen, looking at the photos? There are an awful lot. And can I have water, please? I'm driving, remember.'

'Sure.' He retrieved his glass, poured her water from the chiller in the fridge and sat next to her at the breakfast bar overlooking the sea. 'So, what have we got?'

'Lots.'

There *were* lots, she wasn't exaggerating. And there were gaps in the numbers, all over the place.

'What happened to the others? There are loads missing.'

'I deleted them.'

He blinked. 'Really? That's not like you. You never throw anything out.'

'Maybe you don't know me as well as you think,' she said.

Or maybe you do, she thought, scrolling down through the thumbnails and registering just how many she'd removed and saved elsewhere.

'Just start at the top,' he suggested, so they did.

Him laughing on the plane. She loved that one. Others in their suite, in the pool—still too many of them, although she'd taken bucket-loads out for what she'd called her private collection.

Self-indulgent fantasy, more like.

She knew what she was doing. She was building a memory bank, filling it with images to sustain her if it all went wrong.

There were some of her, too, ones he'd taken of her shot against the backdrop of the valley behind their terrace, or with Ella, playing. She'd nearly taken them out, too, but because nearly all of them had Ella in, she hadn't. He could have them for his own use.

'Right, so which ones do you want me to work on?'

He didn't hold back. She got a running commentary on the ones he liked, the ones he couldn't place, the ones he'd have to check with the Valtieri family before they were used.

'How about a *short*list for the blog?' she suggested drily, when he'd selected about two hundred.

He laughed. 'Sorry. These are just the ones I really like. I'll go through them again and be a bit more selective. I was just getting an overview. Why don't you just leave them with me so I'm not wasting your time? Did you copy them?'

She handed him the memory stick with the carefully edited photos that she'd deemed fit to give him. 'Here. Don't lose it. Just make a note and let me know.'

'I will. Thanks. Want the guided tour?'

'Of your furniture? I think I'll pass, if you don't

mind. I still have stuff to do—like writing to all my wedding guests.'

'Sorry. Of course you do. And I've taken your whole day already. Go, and don't rush back in the morning. I should be fine until ten, at least.'

She moved in on Sunday, and the film crew arrived on Monday and brought chaos to the house—lights, reflectors, a million people apparently needed to co-ordinate the shoot, and Ella took one look at it all and started to cry.

Amy ended up taking her home for the day more than once, which would have been fine if they'd stopped filming at her bedtime, but sometimes it dragged on, and then she'd be unsettled, and he'd have to break off and read her a story and sing to her before she'd go back to sleep.

'I'm sorry, this is really tough for you both,' Leo said after a particularly late shoot. 'I didn't know it would disrupt her life so much. I should have thought it through.'

'It's fine, Leo,' she assured him. 'We're coping.'

And they were, just about, but it was like being back in Tuscany, tripping over each other in the kitchen in the morning, having breakfast together with Ella, doing all the happy families stuff that was tearing her apart, with the added bonus of doing it under the eyes of the film crew.

And because of the 'what happened in Tuscany' thing, the enforced intimacy was making it harder and harder to be around each other without touching and she was seriously regretting suggesting it.

Then one night Ella cried and she got up to her, but Leo got there first. 'It's fine. I'll deal with her, you go back to bed,' he said, but the fourth time she woke there was a tap on her door and Leo came in.

'Amy, I think she needs the doctor. She must have an ear infection or something. I have to take her to the hospital. They have an out of hours service there, apparently.'

'Want me to come?'

The relief on his face should have been comical, but it was born of worry, so she threw her clothes on and went with him. It took what felt like hours, of course, before they came home armed with antibiotics and some pain relief, and Leo looked like hell.

'I feel sorry for the make-up lady who's going to have to deal with the bags under your eyes in the morning,' she said ruefully when the baby was finally settled.

'Don't you mean later in the morning?' he sighed, yawning hugely and reaching for a glass. 'Water? Tea? I've given up on sleep. Decided it's an overrated pastime.'

She laughed softly and joined him. 'Tea,' she said.

'Good idea. We'll watch the sun come up.'

Which wasn't a good idea at all. Tuscany again, and sitting on the terrace overlooking the valley with the swallows swooping. Except here it was the gulls, their mournful cries haunting in the pale light of dawn.

'Thank you for coming with me to the hospital,' he said quietly.

'You don't have to thank me, Leo. I was happy to do it. I was worried about her.'

She stared out over the sea, watching it flood with colour as the sun crept over the horizon. It was beautiful, and it would have been perfect had she been able to do what she wanted to do and rest her head on his shoulder, but of course she couldn't.

'How's the filming going?' she asked, and he sighed.

'OK, I think, but I'm neglecting the restaurant,

and I haven't even touched the Tuscany blog. On the plus side, we're nearly two weeks in.'

Really? Only six more weeks to go? And when it ended, they'd have no more excuse to be together, so it would be crunch time, and she was in no way ready to let him go. She drained her tea and stood up.

'I might go back to bed and see if I can sleep for a few more minutes,' she said, and left him sitting there, silhouetted against the sunrise. It would have made a good photo. Another one to join the many in her private collection.

She turned her back on him and walked away.

The filming was better after that, the next day not as long, and Leo had a chance to catch up with the restaurant over the weekend. Ella was fine, her ear infection settling quickly, but she'd slept a lot to catch up so Amy had helped him with the blog over the weekend, edited the photos, pulled it all together, and she showed it to him on Monday night after Ella was in bed.

'Oh, it looks fantastic, Amy,' he said, sitting back and sighing with relief. 'Thank you so much. The photos are amazing.'

'Better than your selfies?' she teased lightly, and he laughed.

'So much better!' He leant over and kissed her fleetingly, then pulled away, grabbing her by the hand and towing her into the kitchen. 'Come on, I'm cooking you dinner.'

'Is that my reward?'

'You'd better believe it. I have something amazing for you.'

'That poor lobster that's been crawling around your sink?'

'That was for filming. This is for us. Sit.'

She sat, propped up at the breakfast bar watching him work. She could spend her life doing it. What was she thinking? She *was* spending her life doing it, and it was amazing. Or would be, if only she dared to believe in it.

'The producer was talking about a cookery book,' he told her while he worked. 'Well, more a lifestyle-type book. Like the blog, but more so, linking it to the series. It would make sense, and of course they've got stills they've taken while I've been working so it should be quite easy.'

So he wouldn't need her. She stifled her disappointment, because she was pleased for him anyway. 'That sounds good.'

'I thought so, too.'

He was still chopping and fiddling. 'Is it going to be long? I'm starving,' she said plaintively.

'Five minutes, tops. Here, eat these. New amuse-bouche ideas for the restaurant. Tell me what you think.'

'Yummy,' she said, and had another, watching him as she ate the delicious little morsels. The steak was flash-fried, left to rest in the marinade while he blanched fresh green beans, and then he crushed the new potatoes, criss-crossed them with beans, thinly sliced the steak and piled it on before drizzling the marinade over the top.

'There. Never let it be said that I don't feed you properly. Wine?'

He handed her a glass without waiting for her reply, and she sipped it and frowned.

'Is this one of the Valtieri wines?'

'Yes. It goes well, doesn't it?'

'Mmm. It's gorgeous. So's the steak. It's like butter it's so tender.'

'What can I say? I'm just a genius,' he said, grinning, and hitched up on the stool next to her, and it would have been so natural, so easy to lean towards him and kiss that wicked smile.

She turned her attention back to her food, and

ignored her clamouring body. Let it clamour. They had to play it his way, and if that meant she couldn't push him, so be it. He was turning his life around, getting it back on track, and she wasn't going to do anything to derail his rehabilitation. Or her own.

And Leo was definitely derailing material.

'Coffee?' he asked when she'd finished the crème brûlée he'd had left over from filming today.

'Please.'

And just because they could, just because it was Leo's favourite thing in the world to do at that time of day, they took it outside on the deck and sat side by side on the steps to drink it.

He'd turned the lights down in the kitchen, so they were sitting staring out across the darkened garden at the moonlit sea. Lights twinkled on it here and there, as the lights had twinkled in Tuscany, only here they were on the sea, and the smell of salt was in the air, the ebbing waves tugging on the shingle the only sound to break the silence.

She leant against him, resting her shoulder against his, knowing it was foolish, tired of fighting it, and with a shaky sigh he set his cup down, turned his head towards her and searched her eyes, his arm drawing her closer.

'Are we going to be OK, Amy?' he asked, as if he'd read her mind. His voice was soft, a little gruff. Perhaps a little afraid. She could understand that.

'I don't know. I want us to be, but all the time there's this threat hanging over us, the possibility that it won't, that it's just another mistake for both of us. And I don't want that. I want to be able to sit with you in the dark and talk, like we've done before a million times, and not feel this…crazy fear stalking me that it could be the last time.'

She took a sip of her coffee, but it tasted awful so she put it down.

'I'm going to bed,' she said. 'I'm tired and I can't do this any more. Pretend there's nothing going on, nothing between us except an outgrown friendship that neither of us can let go of. It's more than that, so much more than that, but I don't know if I can dare believe in it, and I don't think you can, either.'

She got to her feet, and he stood up and pulled her gently into his arms, cradling her against his chest. 'I'm sorry. Go on, go to bed. I'll see you in the morning.'

He bent and brushed his lips against her cheek,

the stubble teasing her skin and making her body ache for more, and then he let her go.

She heard him come upstairs a few minutes later. He hesitated at her door and she willed him to come in, but he didn't, and she rolled to her side and shut her eyes firmly and willed herself to sleep instead.

The film crew interrupted their breakfast the next morning, but she didn't mind. The place stank of coffee, and she couldn't get Ella out of the house fast enough.

She strapped her into the car seat, pulled off the drive and went into town. They were running short of her follow-on milk formula, so she popped into the supermarket and picked up some up, and then she headed for the seafront. They could go to the beach, she thought, and then they passed a café and the smell of coffee hit her like a brick.

She pressed her hand to her mouth and walked on, her footsteps slowing to a halt as soon as they were out of range. No. She couldn't be. But she could see Isabelle's face so clearly, hear her saying that she couldn't stand the smell of coffee, and last night it had tasted vile.

But—how? She was on the Pill. She'd taken it religiously.

Except for the first day in Tuscany, the Sunday morning. She'd forgotten it then, taken it in the afternoon, about four. Nine hours late. And it was only the mini-pill, because she and Nick had planned to start a family anyway, and a month or so earlier wouldn't have mattered. And she'd hardly seen Nick for weeks before the wedding. Which meant if she was pregnant, it was definitely Leo's baby.

She turned the buggy round, crossed the road and went to the chemist's, bought a pregnancy test with a gestation indicator and went to another café that didn't smell so much and had decent loos. She took Ella with her into the cubicle which doubled as disabled and baby changing, so there was room for the buggy, and she did the test, put the lid back on the wand and propped it up, and watched her world change for ever.

He hadn't seen them all day.

The filming had gone well and the crew had packed up early, but Amy and Ella still weren't home.

Perhaps she'd taken Ella to her mother's, or to

a friend's house? Probably. It was nearly time for Ella to eat, so he knew they wouldn't be long, but he was impatient.

He'd been thinking about what Amy had said last night, about their lives being on hold while they gave themselves time, and he'd decided he didn't want more time. He wanted Amy, at home with him, with Ella, in his bed, in his life. For ever.

Finally the gravel crunched. He heard her key in the door, and felt the fizz of anticipation in his veins, warring with an undercurrent of dread, just in case. What would she say? Would it be yes? Please, God, not no—

'Hi. Have you had a good day?' he asked, taking Ella from her with a smile and snuggling her close.

'Busy,' she said, heading into the kitchen with a shopping bag. 'Where are the film crew?'

'We finished early. So what did you do all day?'

'Oh, this and that. We went to town and picked up some formula, but it was a bit hot so we went to Mum's and had lunch in the garden and stayed there the rest of the day.'

'I thought you might have been there. I was about to ring you. Has she eaten?'

'Not recently. She had a snack at three. Are you OK to take over? I've got a few things I need to do.'

He frowned. He couldn't really put his finger on it, but she didn't sound quite right. 'Sure, you go ahead. Supper at seven?'

'If you like. Call me when you're done, OK? I might have a shower, it's been a hot day.'

She ran upstairs, and he took Ella through to the kitchen, put her in her high chair and gave her her supper. She fed herself and made an appalling mess, but he didn't care. All he could think about was Amy, and what was wrong with her, because something was and he was desperately hoping it wasn't a continuation of what she'd said last night.

What if she turned him down? Walked away and left him?

On autopilot, he wiped Ella's hands and took her up to bath her.

'Amy?'

'Yes?'

He opened her bedroom door and found her sitting up on her bed, the laptop open on her lap. She shut it and looked up at him. 'Is supper ready?'

'It won't take long. Can you come down? I want to talk to you.'

'Sure,' she said, but she looked tense and he wondered why.

'Can I go first?' she said, and he hesitated for a moment then nodded.

'Sure. Do you want a drink?'

'Just water.'

He filled a tumbler from the fridge and handed it to her, and she headed outside to the garden, perching on the step in what had become her usual place, and he crossed the deck and sat down beside her.

She drew her breath in as if she was going to speak, then let it out again and bit her lip.

'Amy? What is it?'

She sucked in another shaky breath, turned to look at him and said, 'I'm pregnant.'

He felt the blood drain from his head, and propped his elbows on shaking knees, the world slowing so abruptly that thoughts and feelings crashed into each other and slid away again before he could grasp them.

'How?' he asked her, his voice taut. He raised his head and stared at her. 'How, Amy? You're on the Pill—I know that, I watched you take it every morning.'

'Not every morning,' she said heavily. 'The first day, I forgot. I didn't take it until the afternoon.'

'And that's enough?'

'Apparently. I didn't even think about it, because it didn't matter any more. I wasn't on my honeymoon, and we weren't—'

He was trying to assimilate that, and then another thought, much harder to take, brought bile to his throat.

'How do you know it's mine?' he asked, and his voice sounded cold to his ears, harsh, uncompromising. 'How do you know it isn't...?' He couldn't even bring himself to say Nick's name out loud, but it echoed between them in the silence.

'Because it's the only time I've taken it late, and because of this.'

She pulled something out of her pocket and handed it to him. A plastic thing, pen-sized or a little more, with a window on one side. And in the window was the word 'pregnant' and beneath it '2-3'.

A pregnancy test, he realised. And 2-3?

'What does this mean?' he asked, pointing to it with a finger that wasn't quite steady.

'Two to three weeks since conception.'

The weekend they'd been alone in the *palazzo*. So it *was* his baby. Then another hideous thought occurred to him.

'When did you do this test?'

'This morning,' she told him, her voice drained and lifeless.

'Are you sure? Are you sure you didn't do it a week or two ago?'

Her eyes widened, and the colour drained from her face.

'You think I'd lie to you about something as fundamental as this?'

'You wouldn't be the first.'

She stared at him for what seemed like for ever, and then she got to her feet.

'Where are you going?'

'Home. To my mother.'

'Not to Nick?'

She turned back to him, her eyes flashing with fury. 'Why would I go running to Nick to tell him I've been stupid enough to let you get me pregnant?' she asked him bluntly. 'If you could really think that then you don't know me at all. It's none of Nick's business. It's my business, and it could have been yours, but if you really think I could lie to you about something so precious, so amazing, so beautiful as our child, then I don't think we have anything left to say to each other. You wanted my terrifying honesty. Well, this is it. I'm sorry you don't like it, but *I am not Lisa*!'

He heard her footsteps across the decking, the vibrations going through him like an earthquake, then the sound of the front door slamming and the gravel crunching under her tyres as she drove off.

He stared blindly after her as the sound of her car faded into the evening, drowned out by the cries of gulls and the soft crash of the waves on the shore below, and then like a bolt of lightning the pain hit him squarely in the chest.

Her mother was wonderful and didn't say a thing, just heard her out, hugged her while she cried and made them both tea.

'Do you know how wonderful you are?' she asked, and her mother's face crumpled briefly.

'Don't be silly. I'm just your mother. You'll know what I mean, soon enough. It'll make sense.'

Her eyes filled with tears. 'I already know. I'm not going to see Ella again, Mum. Never.'

'Of course you will.'

'No, I won't. Or Leo.' Her voice cracked on his name, and she bit her lips until she could taste blood.

'That's a little difficult. He has a right to see his child, you know.'

'Except he doesn't believe it is his child.'

'Are you absolutely certain that it is?'

'Yes,' she said, sighing heavily. 'Nick was away, wasn't he, for five weeks before the wedding. I only saw him a couple of times, and we didn't...'

She couldn't finish that, not to her mother, which was ridiculous under the circumstances, but she didn't need to say any more.

'You ought to eat, darling.'

'I couldn't. I just feel sick.'

'Carbs,' her mother said, and produced a packet of plain rich tea biscuits. 'Here,' she said, thrusting one in her hand. 'Dunk it in your tea.'

Was it really his? Could this really be happening to him again?

He'd sat outside for hours until the shock wore off and was replaced by a sickening emptiness.

The pregnancy test, he thought. Check it out. He went up to her room and opened her laptop, and was confronted by a page of images of him.

Images he'd never seen. Ones she'd lied about deleting. Why? Because she loved him? And he loved her. He could see it clearly in the pictures, and he knew it in his heart.

He searched for the pregnancy test and came up with it.

As accurate as an ultrasound.

Which meant if she *had* just done it, the baby was his—and he'd accused her of lying, of trying to pass another man's baby off as his.

And he knew then, with shocking certainty, that she hadn't lied to him. Not about that. As she'd pointed out at several thousand decibels, she wasn't Lisa. Not in any way. And he owed her an apology.

A lifetime of apologies, starting now.

But he couldn't leave Ella behind, so he lifted her out of her cot, put her in the car and drove to Jill's. Amy's car was on the drive, and he went to the front door and rang the bell.

'Leo.'

'I'm an idiot,' he said, and he felt his eyes filling and blinked hard. 'Can I see her?'

'Where's Ella?'

'In the car, asleep.'

'Put her in the sitting room. Amy's in her room.'

He laid her on the sofa next to Jill, went upstairs to Amy's room and took a deep breath.

'Go away, Leo,' she said, before he even knocked, but he wasn't going anywhere.

He opened the door, ducked to avoid the flying missile she hurled at him and walked towards her, heart pounding.

'Get out.'

'No. I've come to apologise. I've been an idiot. I know you're not Lisa, and I know you wouldn't lie to me about anything important. You've never really lied to me, not even when you knew the truth was going to hurt me. And I know you're not lying now.' He took another step towards her. 'Can we talk?'

'What is there to say?'

'What I wanted to say to you when you got home. That I love you. That I don't want to wait any longer, because I do know you, Amy, I know you through and through, and you know me. We haven't changed that much, not deep down where it matters, and I know we've got what it takes. I was just hiding from it because I was afraid, because I've screwed up one marriage, but I'm not going to screw up another.'

'Marriage?' She stared at him blankly. 'I hate to

point this out to you, but we aren't exactly married. We aren't exactly anything.'

'No. But we should be. We haven't lost our friendship, Amy, but it has changed. Maybe the word is evolved. Evolved into something stronger. Something that will stay the course. We were both just afraid to try again, afraid to trust what was under our noses all the time. We should have had more faith in each other and in ourselves.'

He took her hand and wrapped it in his, hanging on for dear life, because he couldn't let her go. Let them go.

'I love you, Amy. I'll always love you. Marry me. Me and Ella, and you and our baby. We can be a proper family.'

Amy sat down on the edge of her bed, her knees shaking.

'Are you serious? Leo, you were horrible to me!'

'I know, and I can't tell you how sorry I am. I was just shocked, and there was a bit of déjà vu going on, but I should have listened to you.'

'You should. But I knew you wouldn't, because of Lisa—'

'Shh,' he said, touching a finger to her lips.

'Lisa's gone, Amy. This is between you and me now, you and me and our baby.'

'And Ella,' she said.

'And Ella. Of course and Ella. She won't be an only child any more. I was so worried about that.'

'You said it would be a cold day in hell before you got married again,' she reminded him, and his eyes filled with sadness.

'I was wrong. It felt like a cold day in hell when you walked out of my life. Come back to me, Amy? Please? I need you. I can't live without you, without your friendship, your support, your understanding. Your atrocious sense of humour. Your untidiness. The fact that you do lie to me, just a little, on occasions.'

'When?' she asked, scrolling back desperately.

'The photos,' he said with a wry smile on the mouth she just wanted to kiss now. You told me you'd deleted them, but you haven't. They're still on your laptop. I saw them just now. I opened your laptop to check up on pregnancy tests and I found them. Photos of me. Why?'

She closed her eyes. 'It doesn't matter why.'

'It does to me, because I know why I would want photos of you. Why I took them. So I can look at the images when you're gone, and still, in some small way, have you with me. Amy, I'm scared,' he went on, and she opened her eyes and looked up at him again, seeing the truth of it in his eyes.

'I'm scared I'll fail you, let you down like I let Lisa down. My lifestyle is chaotic, and it's not conducive to a happy marriage. How many celebrity chefs—forget celebrity, just normal chefs—are happily married? Not many. So many of their marriages fall apart, and I don't want that to happen to us, but I need you in my life, and I'll have to trust your faith in me, your belief that we can make it work. That I won't let you down.'

'You already have, today. You didn't listen.'

He closed his eyes, shaking his head slowly, and then he looked up, his eyes locking with hers, holding them firm.

'I know. And I'm sorry, but I'll never do it again. I love you, Amy, and I need you, and I've never been more serious about anything in my life. Please marry me.'

He meant it. He really, truly meant it.

She closed her eyes, opened them again and smiled at him. She thought he smiled back, but she couldn't really see any more. 'Yes,' she said softly. 'Oh, yes, please.'

He laughed, but it turned into a ragged groan, and he hauled her into his arms and cradled her against his heart.

'You won't let me down,' she told him. 'I won't let you. Just one more thing—will you please kiss me? I've forgotten what it feels like.'

'I've got a better idea. Ella's downstairs with your mother, and she needs to be back in bed in her own home, and so do I. Come home with us, Amy. It doesn't feel right without you.'

It didn't feel right without him, either. Nothing felt right. And home sounded wonderful.

'Kiss me first?' she said with a smile, and he laughed softly.

'Well, it's tough but I'll see if I can remember how,' he murmured, and she could feel the smile on his lips…

EPILOGUE

'ARE YOU READY?'

Such simple words, but they'd had the power to change the whole course of her life.

Was she ready?

For the marriage—the *lifetime*—with Leo?

Mingling with the birdsong and the voices of the people clustered outside the church gates were the familiar strains of the organ music.

The overture for their wedding.

No. Their *marriage.* Subtle difference, but hugely significant.

Amy glanced through the doorway of the church and caught the smiles on the row of faces in the back pew, and she smiled back, her heart skittering under the fitted bodice that suddenly seemed so tight she could hardly breathe.

The church was full, the food cooked, the champagne on ice. And Leo was waiting for her answer.

Her dearest friend, the love of her life, who'd

been there for her when she'd scraped her knees, had her heart broken for the first time, when her father had died, who'd just—been there, her whole life, her friend and companion and cheerleader. Her lover. And she did love him.

Enough to marry him? Till death us do part, and all that?

Oh, yes. And she was ready. Ready for the chemistry, the fireworks, the amazingness that was her life with Leo.

Bring it on.

She straightened her shoulders, tilted up her chin and gave Leo her most dazzling smile.

'Yes,' she said firmly. 'I'm ready. How about you? Because I don't want you feeling pressured into this for the wrong reason. You can still walk away. I'll understand.'

'No way,' he said, just as firmly. 'It's taken me far too long to realise how much I love you, and I can't think of a better reason to marry you, or a better time to do it than now.'

His smile was tender, his eyes blazing with love, and she let out the breath she'd been holding.

'Well, that's a relief,' she said with a little laugh, and he smiled and shook his head.

'Silly girl. Amy, are you sure you don't want my father to walk you down the aisle? He's quite happy to.'

'No. I don't need anyone to give me away, Leo, and you're the only man I want by my side.'

'Good.You look beautiful, Amy,' he added gruffly, looking down into her eyes. 'More beautiful than I've ever seen you.'

'Thank you,' she said softly 'You don't look so bad yourself.'

She kissed his cheek and flashed a smile over her shoulder at her bridesmaids. 'OK, girls? Good to go?'

They nodded, and she turned back to Leo. 'OK, then. Let's do this,' she said, and she could feel the smile in her heart reflected in his eyes.

'I love you, Amy,' he murmured, and then slowly, steadily, he walked her down the aisle.

And when they reached the chancel steps he stopped, those beautiful golden eyes filled with love and pride, and he turned her into his arms and kissed her.

The congregation went wild, and he let her go and stood back a little, his smile wry.

'That was just in case you'd forgotten what it's like,' he teased, but his eyes weren't laughing, because marrying Amy was the single most important thing he would ever do in his life, and he was going to make sure they did it right.

* * * * *

MILLS & BOON®

Large Print – July 2015

THE TAMING OF XANDER STERNE
Carole Mortimer

IN THE BRAZILIAN'S DEBT
Susan Stephens

AT THE COUNT'S BIDDING
Caitlin Crews

THE SHEIKH'S SINFUL SEDUCTION
Dani Collins

THE REAL ROMERO
Cathy Williams

HIS DEFIANT DESERT QUEEN
Jane Porter

PRINCE NADIR'S SECRET HEIR
Michelle Conder

THE RENEGADE BILLIONAIRE
Rebecca Winters

THE PLAYBOY OF ROME
Jennifer Faye

REUNITED WITH HER ITALIAN EX
Lucy Gordon

HER KNIGHT IN THE OUTBACK
Nikki Logan

0615 Rom LP